GIVE A GHOST A BAD NAME

A REAPER WITCH MYSTERY

ELLE ADAMS

Tonight was the grand opening of our first ghost tour at the Riverside Inn, and there was no sign of any ghosts.

"This might be a problem," I remarked to nobody in particular, since Carey was still at school and I was alone behind the bar with no customers to speak of. Not that unusual for the time before the lunch-hour rush, but even my brother, Mart, was nowhere to be seen. Weird.

I walked out from behind the bar and peered through the transparent doors connecting the restaurant to the Riverside Inn's lobby. On the other side, Allie stood behind the reception desk and handed the latest group of guests the keys to their room. She'd donned her best silver cloak and matching hat in honour of our grand opening and also clipped a pair of small cartoon ghosts to her spectacles. I was willing to bet she wore matching socks, too, like her daughter, Carey. We'd had no shortage of bookings this weekend for our first ghost tour, but we were short on actual ghosts.

Typical of the local spirits to vanish the one time we actually needed them around. Shaking my head, I returned to the bar to wait for the guests to depart for their rooms. While I didn't have to hide my ghost-whispering tendencies anymore, that didn't mean I wanted to broadcast the less-than-glamourous side of wrangling spirits into obedience. I had to at least attempt to maintain the illusion that I knew what I was doing.

Also, if it turned out that I had to make use of my Reaper skills to find them, then few people would be able to watch without being mentally scarred for life, which would be a slight hindrance to our plans for a family-friendly ghost-tour venture. Not to mention I didn't like exposing my half-Reaper status to outsiders if I could help it. Most of the people local to the town of Hawkwood Hollow knew, but I maintained the hope that they wouldn't spread the word any further afield.

Yes, I was aware that helping to run a ghost-tour business was hardly an effective cover story, but both Allie—who owned the inn—and her daughter lacked the ability to see ghosts, let alone perform any Reaper trickery. I was simply there to make sure the ghosts behaved themselves, nothing more.

Pay no attention to the Reaper behind the curtain.

After the guests had departed the lobby, I emerged to search for our elusive spirits.

Allie smiled at me from behind the counter. "Hey, Maura. What're you doing out here?"

"Looking for my brother," I told her.

"He's not around?" She adjusted one of the little ghostly charms on the side of her glasses. "Are you sure he's not haunting the guests?"

"He might be." I'd given him open permission to do all the haunting he liked—within reason—which stood in stark contrast to my usual insistence that he kept his ghostly antics to a minimum. For the first time, the guests knew exactly what they were getting into when they stayed at an inn that was inhabited by ghosts. They'd come for a haunting and expected to get one. "Or he's preparing for the tour."

"He's been looking forward to this, right?"

"To an annoying degree." Over the past few years, my brother had spent a lot of time as the only ghost in the room, and he'd been delighted when I'd agreed to help Carey realise her ambitions to turn the family inn into a haunted hotel. She'd dreamed of doing so for years, but her inability to actually *see* ghosts had put a wedge in her plans until I'd come along—without knowing I'd end up staying, I might add.

When I'd first moved to Hawkwood Hollow, I'd been less than enthused when I'd discovered that the number of ghosts in town outnumbered the living people and that nobody had any intention of getting rid of them. Usually the local Reaper was on hand to banish those spirits to the afterworld, except the town's sole Reaper had gone into early retirement more than two decades prior, after the death of his apprentice, and nobody had stepped in to take his place. No, I certainly wasn't volunteering, not least because I wasn't an official Reaper and I'd frankly rather eat grave dust than come face-to-face with the Reaper Council again.

Eventually, I'd come to accept that Hawkwood Hollow's ghosts weren't going anywhere, and if we could turn the town's one perk into a tourist attraction, then it could only be a good thing. Assuming our ghostly employees showed their faces before tonight.

I approached the games room at the back of the reception area and heard the hum of a TV and several voices behind the closed door. *Aha.*

Sure enough, I pushed open the door to reveal every single one of the inn's resident ghosts, including Mart. The youngest, Vicky, sat in front of the TV, watching cartoons, while Jonathan and Brian played pool at the table. Wade and Louise chattered in the corner, while my brother hovered in mid-air, juggling bits of popcorn, which he dropped all over the floor when he saw me watching him. He swept to his feet and gave a dramatic bow. "Welcome to our domain, sister mine."

"You do realise our guests are already arriving, don't you?" I addressed the room in general. "Are you slacking off?"

"We're strategising," Mart said self-importantly.

"I thought you wanted us to save the haunting for the big tour tonight," added Jonathan, one of the younger ghosts. He looked a few years older than my brother, but appearances could be deceptive with ghosts, who were forever frozen at the age of their death. Mart was eternally stuck at eighteen, which was slightly better than him being stuck as a small child the way Vicky was, but I sometimes wished his maturity level had evolved past his teens.

"I didn't mean you could all hang around in here watching TV," I said. "The guests would be delighted if they got a preview of a little ghostly mischief before the evening. You can build up to the big event with a few small incidents, can't you? Locked doors, mysteriously flickering lights, that sort of thing."

"Testing out all the showers?" Mart asked hopefully.

"Definitely not." He already flooded my room at least once a week if I didn't keep a close eye on him; I'd met dozens of ghosts, and none of them enjoyed hot showers as much as my brother did. "Don't do anything that might cause damage or lead to complaints. Didn't I already tell you that?"

Not that my brother listened to me at the best of times. It was a miracle I'd convinced him to agree to stick to the planned schedule for our ghost tours, but for once in my life, his need for attention had won out over his desire to rebel against my orders.

"Maura," Allie called through the door. "You have customers."

"Oops." To the ghosts, I said, "You can stay in here until closing time if you like, but if I were you, I'd want to get the guests in the mood for tonight's haunting. Have a think about it."

Allie watched from the reception desk as I left the room and closed the door on the ghosts. She'd long since grown used to my habit of appearing to converse with thin air, and I had to admire how swiftly she'd adapted to our incorporeal guests too. Unlike her daughter, Allie had never planned to end up running a haunted attraction. She'd been the sole owner of the inn and restaurant since the death of Carey's father some years ago, and keeping the place running was an impressive enough feat on top of single-parenting a sensitive teenager whose obsession with ghosts had mostly been met with ridicule from her classmates. It gave me no end of satisfaction to know that they regretted their comments now we'd begun to build a successful business out of the town's major ghost problem.

"Everything okay in there?" asked Allie.

"Yeah, the ghosts just needed a reminder that our guests did come here expecting a haunting experience outside of the tour," I explained. "I suggested they should give them a taste of what's to come."

"I don't blame them for saving their best for later," she said. "I have to admit I didn't expect us to get quite this many bookings."

"Your daughter's a whiz at publicity," I reminded her.

"I'd say more credit goes to you for making this happen."

"I'm just your friendly neighbourhood Reaper." Compliments always made me uncomfortable, and besides, it *was* mostly Carey's work. Whenever Allie tried to claim I was the one who'd inspired her to make a go of this, I pointed out that Carey's plans had existed far before my arrival in town. Pure luck had brought me here—that, and a chronic lack of cash. The latter problem had been solved when I'd found permanent employment here in Hawkwood Hollow, and I owed Allie for that. Honestly, it was the least I could do for both of them to help her daughter with her ghost-tour ambitions.

I returned to the restaurant to serve the pair of witches waiting at the bar, who ordered two of our Halloween-all-year-round themed cocktails and complimented the new decorations we'd put up for the grand opening.

"We're here for the ghost tour later," said the taller of the two witches, whose dark hair was buzzed short. "Do you have merchandise? That logo of yours would look great on a T-shirt."

She indicated the cute cartoon ghost that featured in the banners we'd festooned the bar with, which was a product of Carey's impressive rendering of my own terrible drawing into a serviceable logo.

"Not yet," I told her. "We're working on it."

Or Carey was, since my drawing skills amounted to stick people and not much else. I could definitely see her applying her design skills to merchandising, though.

"Fair enough," said the second witch, who sported a pink mohawk.

As I served the witches their drinks—if they wanted to order cocktails at midday, who was I to judge?—Jia, my coworker and fellow ghost-wrangler, entered the restaurant, wearing a T-shirt depicting Boo from Super Mario.

"Hey," I said to her when she joined me behind the bar. "I've already had questions about merchandise. Might need to ask Carey to get a move on with that."

"Or hire someone else," she said. "Carey might be impressive at multitasking, but she's still only one person."

"True." We did need another staff member—a living one, that is—but our job requirements had only grown more specific with the expansion of our business. It'd be tricky to find someone who fitted in with our eclectic workplace *and* could see ghosts too. Considering the town was packed with ghosts, you wouldn't think it was an unreasonable expectation, but Hawkwood Hollow had an unusually low percentage of inhabitants who were able to see their incorporeal neighbours. My current working theory was that anyone with a gift for seeing ghosts moved out of town at the first opportunity, which I didn't exactly blame them for. I'd actively tried to avoid ghosts for most of my adult life… except for Mart, who was stuck with me whether either of us wanted it or not.

Jia adjusted the name badge she wore on her uniform. "Ready for the big show?"

"Yep," I said. "The ghosts are, too, I think."

In the background, I heard them chattering upstairs, having taken my advice to heart and decided to give our guests a small-scale preview of the delights to come.

"Even the town's ghosts who usually stay hidden are coming out to play," said Jia. "I swear I saw a couple I didn't recognise on my way here. I thought they'd moved on to the next world."

"Let's hope they don't decide to come to the inn," I said. "We don't want our tour disrupted by random local ghosts."

"I don't know. It'll make things memorable for our opening night."

"We selected our spirits for a reason," I reminded her. "We don't want to end up playing host to the type of ghosts who like beatboxing at 2:00 a.m."

"You've met one who did that?"

"Mart went through a phase a few years ago," I said. "He was even more annoying than usual, if you can believe it."

She grinned. "I have my doubts."

Jia and I served customers until Carey came home from school, bounding into the restaurant with all the excitement of a toddler in a toy shop. Of everyone, Carey was by far the most excited to finally kick off the opening night, even more so than the ghosts were.

"People have been asking me questions about the tour all day," she told us. "Even one of Cris's friends said she might be interested in coming."

I made a mental note to keep an eye out for Carey's former bullies if they did show up, though I didn't think even they would have the audacity to try to ruin our big event. They'd been quiet over the past few months anyway, following the incident a few months ago when they'd tried to summon their own ghosts and bitten off more than they could chew, and it was difficult for anyone to deny that Carey's new business venture was a hit with the locals.

"We're almost fully booked for tonight," Allie told her daughter. "I might have to start turning people away if they show up later without a reservation."

"Where'd all these people come from?" Carey scanned the restaurant, her eyes wide.

"Your advertising efforts, of course," said Jia. "You plastered the town in posters *and* shared the grand opening announcement online. It's all thanks to you."

Carey's face turned mauve. "That doesn't explain how we had so much interest. I've never had much luck reaching people with my blog posts before."

"Don't sell yourself short," I said. "Your posts had a ton of reach, but the locals are interested too. They appreciate the novelty. How many people total do we have space for on the tour?"

"Thirty, max," said Allie. "Otherwise we'll have issues with overcrowding in the upstairs corridors. I'll set up a waiting list just in case anyone wants to sign up for a later date."

"Good idea," Carey said. "Tell you what, we can eventually start doing three or four tours per night if we start early."

"It's an idea, but don't try to do too much." Tonight was more of a test run, so we could adjust accordingly if need be. "Things might calm down a bit when people figure out this is going to be a regular thing."

"Yes, and we need to hire more staff before we can increase the number of tours we run each day," Allie told her daughter. "Maura and Jia are already working full-time in the restaurant, too, remember?"

"Oh yeah." Her radiant expression faded a little, then brightened again. "Tell you what, if the tour is a hit with the locals, we can see if any of them want to join our staff."

"One thing at a time," Allie said to her. "Oh, and don't forget to do your homework before the tour starts."

That might be a tall order. Carey's excitement couldn't be quenched, and I'd almost started to pick up on some of it by closing time. We'd had three more requests for merchandise from customers, and someone also asked if we were going to expand our tours to cover parts of the town outside the inn. I replied that we were working on it, since Carey had shown an interest in setting up several different types of tours to have on rotation so we'd have a bit more variety. Her ambitions might be stymied by the town's other residents, though. Especially a certain Reaper, who'd no doubt object to us bringing packs of rowdy tourists into the cemetery where he lived. Old Harold preferred to avoid all company, both living and dead.

While Carey went to change out of her mustard-yellow uniform into something a bit more appropriate for a ghost tour, Jia and I closed up the restaurant and then went to make sure the ghosts were all accounted for. All five of our newer employees were in the lobby, but there was one notable absence. Where'd my brother gone this time?

I scanned the restaurant, seeing a lot of living people but no dead ones. Frowning, I approached the bar and ducked behind the counter, where I spotted a transparent figure hiding behind the kitchen door. "Mart?"

"Yes?" He scooted into view, looking slightly abashed.

"What were you doing back there?"

"Tidying."

I raised a brow at him. "Tidying what?"

"Nothing."

What was he up to? Wait. "You don't have stage fright, do you?"

He pouted. "Stop laughing at me."

"I'm not laughing." Though I had to stifle an incredulous snort at the notion of my overconfident brother experiencing a sudden spate of nerves.

"I don't appreciate that." He poked me in the chest, creating the sensation of being prodded with a transparent icicle.

"Oi." I took a step back out of range. "You have no reason to be afraid. Isn't this what you always wanted?"

"No, what I always wanted was to be a professional Sky Hopper player."

I gave him an eye roll. "Nice try. You used to skip out on broomstick lessons the same as everything else."

"It's all right for you," he said huffily. "It's not easy being the star of the show. Everyone's putting all this pressure on us to perform well today, and now I've forgotten how to haunt people at all."

"You're haunting *me* right this instant," I said. "Just be yourself. And believe me, I don't often say that and mean it."

He gave me another poke, which I dodged, and then

scooted out of the kitchen and across the restaurant. Already the guests were congregating in the lobby. Young mingled with old, the majority of the crowd comprised of witches and wizards, since shifters were generally uninterested in anything related to ghosts, at least in my experience. Drew hadn't been able to make our opening night either. The head of the town's police force had a lot of demands on his attention, so I kept my fingers crossed that we wouldn't need his help.

Ahead of the crowd, Carey waited at the foot of the stairs to the upper floor with a microphone in her hand, dressed in her new smart silver cloak and hat to match her mother's. She carried her bright ghost goggles in her free hand, but she didn't need to be able to see ghosts herself to be an effective host. I was pretty impressed, to be honest. I couldn't have handled that level of responsibility when I was a teenager.

The clocks chimed eight. The guests were ready, and the ghosts were ready too. It was time for the tour to officially begin.

2

As the guests jostled each other in their anticipation, chattering among themselves, Carey clapped her hands to get everyone's attention.

"Welcome to the Riverside Inn, Hawkwood Hollow's first and only haunted attraction," she said. "I hope you enjoy the show."

Applause echoed throughout the room as all eyes turned towards her. Jia and I positioned ourselves at the back as if we were part of the scenery, which was the plan. Allie waited behind the desk to help her daughter if need be, but Carey's usual shyness had completely melted away now that she was in her element, and she beamed as the crowd showered her in applause. The two witches who'd been drinking cocktails earlier were particularly enthusiastic, and I hoped they'd behave themselves on the tour, given the alcohol content of those Halloween drinks. Jia and I were supposed to keep the ghosts in line, not the guests.

A clicking noise sounded amid the crowd. I looked for the source and spotted a short, dark-haired wizard standing on tiptoe behind a surly-looking older couple, snapping photos with an old-fashioned camera. *What's he doing?* We hadn't outright forbidden photography, but I hadn't expected anyone to bother taking pictures of ghosts that wouldn't show up on camera. Mildly annoyed, I ducked my head and hoped he'd refrain from photographing the crowd. I didn't need any photos of me floating around the internet, especially in the context of a haunted hotel.

Jia noticed me fidgeting and whispered, "What's up?"

"I'm starting to wish we'd put up a poster forbidding photography," I said out of the corner of my mouth. "That or I should have worn a disguise."

That rule wouldn't stop the guests snapping pictures outside the inn, though, and as a former Reaper who still possessed all my skills and training, I stood in a murky grey area when it came to the strict rules that Reapers were generally forced to comply with. While I wasn't *technically* breaking any rules by helping Carey to run ghost tours, there'd be repercussions if the Reapers thought I was using my abilities in any way. While I had permission to live and work here in Hawkwood Hollow provided I didn't use my Reaper skills in non-emergency situations, that didn't mean said permission came directly from the Reaper Council or from my former community. I could just imagine my dad's expression if he saw my face on the front page of an advert for ghost tours.

"Should I tell him to stop?" Jia asked in a low voice.

"No, it's better not to draw attention."

The guy taking the photos seemed to have zero regard for other people's personal space either, frequently stepping on toes or knocking his elbows into his neighbours in his efforts to get a good shot. Luckily, Carey didn't seem perturbed by his presence, and she led the crowd through the lobby into the restaurant for the next part of the tour. Meanwhile, I was content to stay in the background, a simple enough task when it was the ghosts everyone was here to see.

Several gasps ensued when Vicky darted in and out of the crowd, grabbing people's hands as she did so. From their responses, I deduced that nobody among our guests could see ghosts. Good. That lessened the chance of someone ruining the fun, though I really wished the dude with the camera would take a hint. Several people gave him dirty looks when he waved the lens in front of their faces, but he seemed oblivious.

While Carey spun a tale about the local ghosts, the restaurant lights flickered overhead, courtesy of Wade, whose special gift consisted of using lights to communicate in Morse code. I couldn't understand it myself, but a number of the crowd could, and they grinned and whispered to one another in excitement as they worked out what he was saying. Mart, meanwhile, had got over his stage fright and amused himself by clattering pans in the kitchen and turning taps on and off in the background.

After the crowd departed the restaurant, their next stop was the games room, where Jonathan enthralled everyone with a display of creepy shadows on the walls, followed by a short game of pool with Brian, who also contributed by dropping the temperature at random intervals. Then it was time for them to go upstairs, where we'd volunteered a couple of hotel rooms to be part of the tour, though the ghosts had permission to haunt every guest who'd signed up for it, no matter which room they were staying in.

Louise greeted everyone at the top of the stairs by making the doors randomly open and close to the tune of "Twinkle, Twinkle, Little Star." When Carey asked the crowd to vote on what tune they wanted her to play for them next, Louise's ghostly rendition of "Another One Bites the Dust" resulted in another burst of applause. Vicky continued to slip in and out of the crowd and seize people's hands, which proved a hit too.

By the time we returned downstairs, the only person who didn't look impressed was the guy with the camera, and that was because he was too focused on getting a good shot of the artfully frozen window Brian had created to pay much attention to anything else.

Mart came drifting over to me as the crowd assembled in the lobby again. "Who's the amateur photographer?"

"Haven't a clue," I replied in an undertone. "I wouldn't object if someone ruined his shot, though."

"Challenge accepted." He sashayed across the lobby and opened the window in front of the photographer, causing a gust of wind to hit him square in the face. I swallowed a laugh at the photographer's incredulous expression, especially when the window promptly slammed and sprayed him with shattered bits of ice.

"What're you looking at?" he said defensively when he saw me looking at him.

I levelled him with a glare. "For what purpose are you taking all those photos, exactly? I didn't think ghosts appeared on camera, so it seems like a waste of time."

"You don't know who I am?" He gave a soft noise of incredulity. "I'm Parker Maven, owner of the Dead Serious blog, where I post my ghost-tour reviews."

"No, I haven't heard of you." Carey might have, since she was more tuned in to the current ghost blogger community than I was. "You should have told Carey. She'd have given you an interview."

"I'm not interested in interviewing anyone," he said. "You work here, do you?"

"Yes." I didn't elaborate, since giving away my Reaper status to a guy with a camera would have been a bad idea even if he hadn't had a major attitude problem. I didn't know if he was really as influential as he seemed to think he was, but you'd think the fact that he couldn't see ghosts would be an impediment to his ability to find decent hauntings. Granted, Carey couldn't see them either, but she at least had Jia and me to point her in the right direction. She also didn't walk onto other people's ghost tours and start snapping photos of the place without asking permission.

"He has to advertise our tour company on his blog, then," Mart said. "Seems only fair that we get some publicity out of this."

Good point. I opened my mouth to ask the guy if he planned on linking to our website and then took a sharp step back when he pointed the camera in my direction. "What are you doing?"

"Taking photos of the scenery," Parker said. "You're in the way."

Man, this guy was annoying. "You know, it's common courtesy to *ask* before taking photos of someone."

Parker ignored me and lifted the camera again, but Mart loudly clapped his hands behind his ears. The blogger startled, fumbling the camera, and gave me an accusing look as he caught it between his fingertips. "If you break my camera, then you'll have to pay for the damage."

"I didn't do anything," I said. "You're the one who came to a haunted inn. What did you expect?"

I walked away before the situation could escalate any further, with my brother cackling away in the background.

When I reached her side, Jia snagged my arm. "What was that about?"

"Do you know that guy?" I whispered. "Parker Maven. Supposedly he's a ghost blogger and a big deal."

"Why would another ghost blogger come here?" she queried.

"Exactly what I was thinking," I said. "I don't want him plastering photos of me all over the internet either."

Maybe I'd been a bit hostile, but I had a lot of very good reasons not to want people randomly snapping photos of me. Besides, his attitude left much to be desired.

"Everyone!" Carey spoke from the foot of the stairs, the microphone projecting her voice across the lobby. "I'd like to thank you all for coming to our opening night. Please leave a review on our website if you can, and for those of you staying at the inn, I hope you enjoy the rest of your visit. Now, let's all give a final round of applause to our ghosts."

The doors to the lobby flew open and the ghosts came streaming back in. Mart zipped over to join them and gave several elaborate bows to the crowd. I'd forgotten Carey wanted to add this extra part onto the end of the tour to round it off, but applause rang out, and cheers echoed off the ceiling.

Such was the noise that I didn't hear the screaming until the clapping began to peter out and everyone's attention turned towards the area next to the restaurant doors—and the older couple I'd seen earlier. The man had collapsed, and from beside him, the woman—presumably his wife—let out another shrill scream. "Someone help!"

Allie made her way over to her, hindered by the crowd stirring around her, while the ghosts fled the lobby and caused another gust of wind to blow open all the windows and doors. I hastened to close the nearest window while Jia moved to help clear Allie's path through to the elderly couple. Carey stood with her microphone hanging limply from her hand, cut off from the rest of us by the restless crowd, and my heart sank into my shoes.

The old woman's voice rang out shrilly from beside a stunned-looking Allie. "He's dead!"

Oh no.

Jia already had her phone in her hand, presumably calling an ambulance, but someone needed to take charge of the restless crowd if we wanted the emergency services to be able to get into the building. Since Carey appeared too stunned to speak, the job fell to me.

"Everyone into the restaurant!" I called out, catching Carey's eye in the hopes that she'd recover from her shock long enough to use her microphone to get everyone's attention. She didn't, which I could hardly blame her for, but luckily, Allie moved in to help me out.

Within minutes, we'd herded everyone into the restaurant —with the exception of the elderly witch, who crouched beside her husband in the doorway.

"How'd he die?" I whispered to Allie.

"Heart attack, I think." Her expression was grave. "Jia called an ambulance, but we might need Drew's help too."

"On it." I reached for my phone and then backed towards the front door as I made the call. If Drew hadn't been at work, he'd already have been here, but there was no help for it.

To my relief, he answered the phone right away. "Maura," he said. "Is the tour over?"

"Yeah… but we have a problem."

"The sort that you need the police for?"

"Unfortunately."

He groaned. "How did I guess?"

"This guy dropped dead of an apparent heart attack," I explained. "We've already called an ambulance, but we're having a little trouble keeping the crowd under control."

Also, if the worst-case scenario turned out to be true and his death *hadn't* been a heart attack or accidental at all, then we didn't need anyone sneaking off before the police could get a handle on the situation. The fact that I needed to consider that possibility at all said a lot about my current track record, but in my experience, it was generally better to cover all our bases.

"I'll be right there."

He ended the call, and I went to wait in the restaurant with Jia. We watched the crowd while Allie tried to comfort Carey. The teenager hadn't said a word yet, her shoulders hunched and her gaze fixed on her own hands.

We didn't have to wait long before the emergency services arrived in a rustle of cloaks. In a town this small, most people didn't own cars, so the paramedics used transportation spells to appear directly in front of the inn. My heart gave a jolt of recognition when I spotted the new coven healer among them—Cathy, who'd once worked under Mina Devlin before the coven leader had fled town after being exposed for covering up three murders—but she barely spared me a glance.

Allie moved in to explain the situation to the paramedics, who converged on the elderly man. Not to mention his widow, who was rapidly dissolving into hysterics.

"What do you mean, an accident?" she shrieked at one of the paramedics. "He was scared to death. The ghosts killed him."

My stomach lurched, and I waited with bated breath for Allie to finish talking to the paramedics before I approached her. An equally tearful Carey hurried to her mother's side, and Allie wrapped an arm around her.

"Please tell me they confirmed it was natural causes," I whispered to Allie.

"They did," she said. "There's little doubt that it was a heart attack, but his wife... well... she wasn't entirely convinced. She seems to think..."

"She—she thinks a ghost did it," Carey mumbled.

Oh no. If there was the slightest chance she was right, it certainly wasn't one of *our* ghosts, but they'd all fled in a panic earlier and I'd have to wait until the crowd had dispersed to track them down. Mart, the sole exception, hovered beside the doors, unusually subdued.

After a few minutes, Drew arrived with a couple of his staff members in tow. From the state of his rumpled dark hair, I assumed he'd run here directly from the police station. While he'd have arrived much sooner if he'd shifted into his werewolf form, he couldn't shift without losing his clothes, which wouldn't exactly be appropriate in this situation. And I was saying that as someone who got to see him naked on a not-infrequent basis too.

"The paramedics confirmed the man died of a heart attack," I told Drew when I met him at the door. "The trouble is… well, his widow doesn't seem to agree."

Concern flickered in his eyes. "You didn't have the tour participants sign a health and safety form before coming in?"

"No, because they were walking around an inn, not going skydiving." I'd have to mention that idea to Carey afterwards, when things had calmed down a little. Right now, she was glued to her mother's side, sobbing silently.

The snap of a camera drew my gaze like a hawk. "Not that guy again. Give me a second."

I marched over to the camera-wielding blogger. "That's enough of that. Have a little respect for the dead, won't you?"

"That's a little hypocritical coming from someone who runs ghost tours," Parker said in a snooty tone.

"Excuse me?" There were several expletives I might have added, but I refrained in case his camera had a recording function turned on. "Respect the living, then. Like his widow."

Not to mention Carey, who would be horrified to be caught on camera sobbing as her business fell apart around her ears. She didn't deserve this guy's disrespect on top of everything else.

Parker shrugged, unimpressed. "That's what you get for being amateurs. You'll all be out of a job by the end of the week."

My hands curled into fists. "Would you like to continue this conversation elsewhere? Like at the bottom of the river?"

"I can assist," Mart told him from behind, which of course he didn't hear.

Parker sniffed and walked away with his nose in the air, while I returned to Drew's side.

Drew gave me a questioning look. "Made a friend, did you?"

"That guy is about to earn himself a lifelong ban from the inn," I growled under my breath. "He's been snapping photos of the body to post on his public blog, as if it's remotely appropriate."

"I'll have a word with him." Drew made to follow Parker, but at that moment, the hysterical widow spotted him and raised her voice.

"Excuse me! Police! My husband was murdered by a ghost!"

Oh, for crying out loud. How could I talk sense into someone who'd just lost her husband in a horrifically public manner? I wasn't exactly a master of tact at the best of times, after all, so I stood back to let Drew handle this one. He retained a calm expression as she ranted, hurling insults at Allie, the inn, and the town as a whole. I didn't hear his reply, but when the paramedics came to ask if she'd like her husband to be taken to the local hospital, Drew seized the chance to escape back to my side.

"Does she actually think he was killed by a ghost?" I asked him. "Because if she does, we're going to have a problem. I might add that none of our ghosts were anywhere near him at the time, but since most people can't see them..."

"She might have a change of heart when she calms down," he said. "Ah—did she have a room reserved at the inn?"

"Good question," I said. "I'll have to check with Allie."

As for our amateur photographer, I'd sooner take a short dive into the river myself than let him stay under the same roof as us, but it wouldn't improve the situation if we decided to kick him out and ended up with two angry guests instead of one.

Regardless, our grand opening night had been memorable for exactly the wrong reasons... and if Parker turned out to be right, then it might well be our last.

3

"We're screwed," Carey said in dismal tones.

She, Allie, and I sat at a table in the restaurant after a sleepless night, waiting for the inevitable moment the guests began coming downstairs to the breakfast buffet. It'd taken long enough to convince them to vacate the lobby the previous night, and I could only imagine how many rumours had proliferated overnight.

"Yeah, you're kinda screwed," Mart put in from behind me. I was incredibly glad the others couldn't hear him because the mood was dire enough already. Carey had spent half the previous night in floods of tears, and while Allie had managed to calm her down, we had yet to formulate a plan to dig our way out of this one.

"Don't be ridiculous," said Allie. "Everyone saw that that man's death was an accident. There's no way to misinterpret it."

"People are saying he was frightened to death by the ghosts," she said despondently. "We can't prove otherwise, can we?"

"I haven't heard anyone who actually believes that," I said.

"Except his widow, and she might have second thoughts when she's had time to process what happened last night."

She wasn't local, so she'd have spent the night in the hospital and would no doubt come back to the inn to claim a refund for her room at some point. I wasn't optimistic enough to believe we'd be let off the hook, but I kept my fingers crossed underneath my seat that she'd take the rumours with her when she left town.

"I certainly wasn't near him when he died," said my brother. "It was pure bad luck if you ask me."

"Is anything just bad luck when it comes to our track record?" At Carey's alarmed expression, I added, "I'm not saying it was a ghost. Trust me, Jia or I would have seen."

The trouble was that we *hadn't* been paying as much attention as we could have been, having let down our guard as the tour had seemed to come to a successful end. We'd faced so many hurdles on the way to setting up our business, from the town's unsavoury history to Carey's age and lack of experience, but when our bookings had exceeded all expectations, I'd let myself hope.

Now, though… a death on our first night, even an accidental one, would cast a shadow over any future business we tried to do. There was no way around it. Jia had gone home in the early hours of the morning, and today was supposed to be her day off, which left it up to the rest of us to defend the inn against irritating photographers and hysterical widows alike.

"Would the others take our word over hers?" Carey whispered. "Most people can't see ghosts, so how can we possibly prove one of them didn't kill him?"

"He did sign up for a ghost tour," said Mart, who was entirely too talkative this morning. "Just saying."

I shot him a warning look. "It wasn't any of our ghosts. There's no evidence whatsoever."

"It's going to show up in every single one of our reviews," Carey went on. "Every single article, blog post, and video will feed the rumour. There's no way to stop it. People love a scandal."

Some people do, unfortunately. I thought of that blogger, Parker Maven, and my hands curled into fists under the table.

"They might not," Allie said. "They'll be reviewing the tour itself, and everyone had a great time."

"That's not going to erase the fact that they saw someone die." Carey's eyes brimmed over with tears. "Even if it was an accident, his safety was our responsibility, wasn't it?"

"We couldn't have prevented it," Allie said. "Maura suggested we ask future guests to sign a health and safety form, which I think is a good idea, but that doesn't mean we're likely to get into any trouble."

"Future guests?" She gave a faint sob. "Why would anyone want to stay here after this? Everything we worked for is ruined."

"It isn't," I insisted. "Trust me, you gave the guests a great experience on the tour, and one unfortunate incident is not going to stop them from coming back. If that widow keeps on hysterically yelling about murder, we might have to come up with a public statement to counter the rumours, but she has no evidence in favour of her theory."

Carey didn't look convinced, but Allie gave her shoulder a reassuring squeeze as she rose to her feet. "I should go and wait by the desk in case anyone wants to check out early. I know it's hard, Carey, but try to focus on the next tour. The other guests need our attention too."

"They do," I said to Carey. "Trust me, this isn't going to be the end of our business."

It was anyone's guess as to what impact yesterday's events would have on the inn's reputation and on bookings for the next few tours, but I didn't believe we were finished. We'd fought too hard for everything to be undone with a single misfortune.

The restaurant was quiet at this hour, most of the guests having slept in, but the majority would be leaving the inn later that day, including a certain blogger. I kept an eye out for trouble as I sipped my coffee, while Carey slumped back in her seat, fiddling with her phone. Then she sat bolt upright, the phone falling from her grip and sliding onto the floor.

"What is it?" I reached for the phone under the table, scooped it up, and handed it back to her.

Carey put the phone back on the table, her hands shaking. "My mum told me not to check, but I saw—I saw we already have two reviews."

"Really?" I peered at the screen when she showed me. "They're both five stars, Carey. And they don't mention that guy's death at all."

"It's only a matter of time before someone does," she mumbled. "Like that Parker guy."

"Is he really as big a deal as he thinks he is?"

"I know who he is." She twisted her hands anxiously under the table. "He has three thousand followers, and he's been interviewed on *Hannah's Hauntings*."

"Ah." Maybe I should have sent Mart to 'accidentally' break his camera overnight, but he might well have sued us for damages if I had. Regardless of his lack of respect for anyone, living or otherwise, he was still technically a guest of the inn. Either way, he was guaranteed to post a review, and it was unlikely to be charitable, given our argument the previous day.

"Exactly." She made to grab her phone, and I caught her wrist before her fingers touched the screen.

"No more reading reviews," I told her sternly. "Focus on

planning the next tour instead."

"I don't want to even think about the next one."

"Then do something fun today," I told her. "We can have a movie night later. I'll check with the ghosts."

I hadn't actually seen any of them except for Mart since the incident the previous night, and I was pretty sure they'd been avoiding the guests on purpose in case anyone else suffered an act of misfortune.

"All right." Carey pocketed her phone and rose to her feet, leaving her breakfast untouched. "I'll be in my room."

After she'd gone, I figured I might as well find our missing ghosts. Mart drifted behind me as I left the restaurant for the inn's lobby and opened the door to the games room, which had become the ghosts' unofficial hangout spot. Our guests rarely used the dusty pool table or the battered dartboard, but the spirits found them endlessly entertaining. Today, however, there was no sign of them.

"I did as you asked me to and kept haunting the guests overnight," Mart told me. "I flicked some lights on and off and turned someone's hot water off when they were taking a shower. You haven't thanked me for it yet, I notice."

"That's because it was my shower, Mart."

"Oops."

"Seriously, where is everyone?" I scanned the deserted games room. "I realise they had a scare yesterday, but we can't run a haunted inn without any ghosts."

"What am I, a piece of furniture?" Mart wanted to know.

"You know that's not what I meant."

He looked even more affronted when I held up a hand to silence his protest, hearing more voices in the lobby. When I backed out of the games room, I found the two witches who'd asked about merchandise the previous day talking to Allie. Both of them wore dark glasses and looked a little worse for wear after yesterday's cocktails, but they were chatting animatedly.

"We'll be sure to recommend you," the witch with the buzzed hair told Allie. "Your daughter has a career in theatre ahead of her."

Allie beamed. "I'll be sure to tell her you said that. It'll mean a lot to her."

"My pleasure," she said. "Do you have business cards I can hand out to other people who might be interested in booking a tour?"

"Oh, of course." She rummaged in her desk drawer. "You really don't have to, but it's appreciated."

"We'll be sure to counter any negativity you might get from the incident after yesterday's tour," said the witch with the pink mohawk. "See you soon."

As they left the inn, I approached Allie at the desk. "At least we have some satisfied customers."

"Some." Her smile faded a little. "I won't mention the three who cancelled their tickets for next week's tours."

I winced. "Yeah, best not to tell Carey that. I already had to warn her not to check our reviews on the website."

"I told her that earlier, but I don't blame her for being anxious to know what people thought."

"Have you seen Parker Maven yet?"

"Who?"

"The guy with the camera," I explained. "He's a blogger and supposedly a big deal, and he and I had a minor altercation yesterday over him snapping photos of that dead guy."

"He didn't, did he?"

"Yeah, his manners are non-existent, but unfortunately he has a platform online," I said. "If any bad publicity shows up, it'll be from his direction."

"How big a platform does he have?" Worry underlaid her tone.

"Ah… three thousand followers, according to Carey, but given his overly inflated sense of self-importance, half of them might be family members or friends."

She sucked in a breath. "Still."

Both of us swivelled towards the automatic doors when they slid open again and none other than the widow of the unfortunate elderly wizard entered. Frown lines covered her face, her curly white hair was in disarray, and her handbag waved from her arm as if she intended to use it to knock out anyone who got into her path. *Oh boy.*

"I don't appreciate you not answering your phone," she said to Allie.

"I was helping another guest, Esther," Allie said. "Can I help you?"

"You can start by paying compensation," the witch—Esther—spat. "My husband died on your property."

"I've already issued you a full refund, with extra added on for the inconvenience—"

"I don't care about any of that," she said. "It's justice I want. Jonas died due to your neglect, and I refuse to let his death go unpunished."

"We already offered to give you anything you request," Allie said. "I appreciate the situation you're in, but nobody on our staff is in any way responsible for what happened to your husband."

"He was a guest at your inn," she said. "A ghost in your employ scared him to death."

"It wasn't a ghost," I said, unable to help myself. "Our ghosts weren't anywhere near your husband."

She gave a disbelieving huff. "And who might you be?"

"Maura," I said. "I trained the ghosts on our team myself. None of them caused your husband's death."

"Empty words," she said. "I saw him die with my own

29

eyes, and there were ghosts in the room at the time, weren't there?"

"Yes, because they were doing their jobs," I said. "This is a haunted inn. I assumed you knew there were ghosts here when you booked your rooms."

She flushed bright red. "If you are in any way insinuating that I or my husband are to blame for his death—"

"I wasn't insinuating anything." I could see Allie signalling to me to quieten down, but I had Esther's attention and I refused to back down. "I was simply pointing out that the ghosts being present in the lobby didn't make them responsible for his death. The police and hospital staff confirmed he died of natural causes, didn't they?"

"That means nothing to me," she said. "I've heard some very unsavoury things about this town in the past day, young lady, and in light of the corruption in your history, I shouldn't be surprised that the rest of the town would close ranks to protect your business."

What was that supposed to mean? "I haven't a clue what you're talking about. Nobody is closing ranks around anyone. We're an independent business."

It was a good job she didn't know I was dating the head of the local police force, but really, the amount of influence I actually had was laughable. The coven had once ruled supreme until I'd driven the leader out of town, but if anything, Mina Devlin's absence had caused people to shun our business, not support us.

"A likely story," she said. "I'm hearing stories of missing coven leaders and mysterious deaths, and frankly I should have expected something like this to happen."

To my alarm, I heard footsteps upstairs, indicating more guests were coming out of their rooms. The last thing we needed was for Esther's irrational tirade to gain an audience.

Allie cleared her throat. "Like I said, I'm willing to assist you with transporting your husband's body home and with anything else you request, but I have a duty to my other guests."

"You have a duty to give me answers," said Esther. "My husband is dead, and your ghosts are responsible. There will be consequences for this, mark my words."

She walked out of the automatic doors, which closed behind her, and I let out a breath.

"Sorry," I said to Allie. "I shouldn't have said that."

"I doubt it would have made a difference if you were polite to her," she said. "She's out for blood, and who can blame her?"

"I can," Mart put in. "She's a menace."

"She's after the ghosts, who can't argue directly with her," I said to him and Allie at the same time. "Speaking of whom, they've all gone into hiding, so I need to find them."

"Go ahead," Allie said. "I'll be fine."

Hoping Esther didn't come back while I was searching the inn, I returned to the games room for another look around. Glimpsing movement under the pool table, I crouched down and found Vicky had curled up into a transparent ball, her arms wrapped around her knees.

"It's just me," I said to her. "C'mon out, it's fine."

"No, it's not fine," she whimpered. "He died. That man died."

"It was an accident," I said. "Really, it's not your fault or anyone else's. Where are the other ghosts, do you know?"

"I don't know."

They'd all likely fled in a panic the same as she had, but they wouldn't have gone far from the inn, surely. I had enough time to round them up, since the next tour wasn't until Tuesday, but it took me a full twenty minutes to coax Vicky out from underneath the pool table, and by the time I emerged, several more guests had come downstairs.

Upon seeing the queue at the breakfast buffet through the transparent doors to the restaurant, I whispered to Vicky, "Go on, grab a hand or two."

"I don't want to scare anyone to death again," she whispered.

"That's not what happened, trust me," I whispered back. "They came here *wanting* to be haunted. Don't you want to end their trip on a good note? Give them something to remember us by?"

She didn't move, but a few people looked in my direction. I caught the word *Reaper*, and my heart gave a lurch. It was a very good job they hadn't used that word when Esther had been accusing us of conspiring to murder her husband. I didn't *think* any of these people agreed with her—they wouldn't have stayed at the inn if they did—but exposing my Reaper status wouldn't exactly help our defence against Esther's irrational accusations.

I ignored their muttering and gave Vicky an encouraging nod, and she scooted forwards into the restaurant. Delighted exclamations of "The ghost girl is back!" followed, and I high-fived her when she returned to the lobby.

"See?" I said. "Nothing to worry about. Our next tour will go ahead as planned."

Vicky's shy smile slipped away. "Not if the others don't come back."

"We'll find them."

As for the guests, most of them would be either going home or leaving the inn to explore the town on their free day, though there was nothing else to do in the area aside from walking in gloomy fields in the rain. There weren't even any other tourist attractions or historical monuments, since the town's only historical event of note was one that the witches would rather everyone forget about. Namely, the flood twenty years ago, the initial cause of the town being overrun with ghosts, and after which everyone had given up on the town ever being anything but a shadow of its former self.

Almost everyone. Allie and Carey thought otherwise, and I knew their business had to come back from this. I'd help ensure it myself.

4

The other ghosts remained elusive despite my best efforts to track them down, so I put on my work uniform and took up my usual position behind the bar for my shift. Vicky retreated into the games room again when the first non-ghost-tour customers showed up, and I persuaded Mart to keep an eye on her to make sure she didn't go back into hiding.

I hadn't seen a certain blogger and amateur photographer yet either, though I seized the opportunity to ask Allie if she'd seen him when she ducked into the restaurant to check up on me partway through my shift.

"He left," she answered. "Left his keys in the corridor and went out the back door without checking out."

"Wonderful." I'd have gone to see if he was still lurking around snapping photos of the inn, but as the only person working behind the bar, I had to keep all our customers happy as well as watching for trouble. At least yesterday's incident didn't seem to have affected the restaurant's popularity, but would that change if word of Esther's accusations spread around the town? So far only three people had asked me about the guy who'd died, and they sounded more curious than anything, so the locals hadn't blacklisted us as a result of the unfortunate incident. Yet.

Drew entered the restaurant at the start of my lunch break, during which I'd intended to make another attempt at tracking down the missing ghosts. I greeted him with a kiss, my mood already improving. "It's good to see you."

"Likewise." He scanned the restaurant, taking in the banners adorning the walls. "Did Carey make those?"

"Yep." I assumed he'd been too occupied with Esther's tirade yesterday to notice the décor. "Have you heard from our favourite bereaved widow?"

"Yes, she called the office and berated our receptionist," he said. "I had to step in to talk to her, which was thoroughly unpleasant. I heard she was a nightmare to the hospital staff too."

"Typical," I said. "She's also threatening our business even though Allie has already offered her a refund and is going out of her way to give her everything she wants."

He grimaced. "Yes, she seems convinced that her husband's death wasn't an accident and won't accept any alternatives."

"I know," I said. "I told her the ghosts weren't anywhere near him, but she wasn't buying it."

"She didn't know?"

"That I'm a Reaper?" I shook my head. "No, and I have no intention of enlightening her. I don't need to give her another angle from which to attack us. Next she'll start claiming that I reaped his soul. It already looks as if we're going to get a ton of publicity over this, and not the good sort either."

"Is Carey okay?"

"She's upset," I said. "As you'd expect. Even the nice reviews we've had so far haven't cheered her up, and I haven't even told her about Esther's visit yet. Honestly, I can't figure out what she hopes to achieve from this. Even if one of the ghosts *did* frighten her husband to death, it's not as if there'd be any way to prove it."

"Exactly," Drew said. "Don't worry, Maura. She can't prosecute anyone based on unproven claims."

"She can still try to shut us down, though." I pulled a face. "She thinks we're to blame for reckless endangerment or something. Can she actually sue us?"

"Depends how much money she has."

"More than us, knowing our luck." The inn had been limping along for years, and from what I'd deduced from Allie, the only reason it had survived this long was because she'd inherited the property from her own relatives. But there were other expenses, and while the restaurant had its steady base of customers, we'd had a recent shaky period following the departure of the coven leader, when the local witches had avoided us in protest. It was typical that we'd run headfirst into another incident that threatened to ruin our image in the eyes of the locals *and* the rest of the magical world at large.

"I doubt she'd want to deal with the hassle," he said. "Once she's occupied with the task of arranging her husband's funeral and sorting out his affairs, she'll calm down."

"I hope you're right." I yawned, going to fix myself another coffee in the hopes that it'd help me stay awake. "I need to find the other ghosts too. They went into hiding after the incident yesterday."

"I'd offer to keep an eye out, but..."

"I know." Drew couldn't see them, like pretty much everyone else. "Want to come over later? I'm going to talk the others into having a movie night."

"Sure," he answered. "Just as long as you don't let the ghosts pick the film again."

"Hey, Mart has good taste at least," I said. "Don't tell him I said that, though."

We'd come up with a rotating schedule of who got to pick the weekly movies so everyone would get a turn, but there were downsides. Mart always picked *Star Wars* or an old episode of *Doctor Who*, which I was always up for, but Vicky invariably picked *My Little Pony*, and Wade liked dreary black-and-white films in which nothing happened.

"I hope Carey cheers up," Drew said. "Anyway, I should go. I'll drop by later."

"Sure thing." I kissed him goodbye and returned to making my coffee. Seeing him always boosted my mood, though it disconcerted me that Esther had gone as far as to contact the police as well as threatening Allie herself. Despite the possible legal implications of someone dying on our property, you couldn't arrest a ghost for murder, or manslaughter, or whatever applied in this situation. If the situation *did* escalate, Allie would take the heat, most likely, since she was the inn's owner. It wasn't fair in the slightest, and I wished there was something I could do to spare her from the blame.

I went to the games room and persuaded Mart to help me find the elusive ghosts by letting him choose the movie for that night.

"Today feels like a *Star Wars* day," he announced. "You've already searched downstairs, so I bet they're hiding in the guests' rooms."

"You can search the ones that are occupied by guests," I said. "I'll look in the empty ones."

We found Jonathan by accident after Mart spotted him outside from an upstairs window, hovering in a corner of the backyard behind the inn. I headed downstairs and through the door at the back of the kitchen, where I spied the ghost's pale form semi-camouflaged against the brick wall.

"What are you doing out here?" I asked him.

"Not much. Being dead."

"Ha." I frowned. "Seriously, I've been running around looking for you since yesterday."

"Why?"

"Because you and all the other ghosts ran off, and I want to make sure we have enough staff for the next tour."

"There's no tour, is there?"

"Of course there is." Why was he acting so weirdly? He still hadn't moved from his spot near the back wall, though it wasn't much of a hiding spot. Admittedly, death couldn't be much fun to witness even from the other side of the afterworld, but still. "We haven't cancelled the next tour, if that's what you mean. You know that guy's death was an accident, right?"

"No."

"What do you mean, no?" A shiver ran down my spine, and when he didn't answer, I pressed on. "Jonathan... what do you mean by that?"

He shook his head, not elaborating. I glanced over at my brother, but Mart seemed as clueless as me as to what was bothering his fellow ghost.

"Jonathan, we've had the man's widow in here threatening Allie and me and accusing us of murder," I told him. "Do you really mean to say it wasn't an accident? Because if it's true, we need to know exactly what happened."

"I don't..." He spoke in a whisper, so I had to strain my ears to catch the words. "I don't know for sure, but I saw a... a shadow."

"Where?" My heart missed a beat. In Reaper business, shadows were generally bad news. I hadn't been looking closely at the man who'd died, so it was entirely possible that I'd missed something, but I fervently hoped that he was mistaken.

"Behind him," he murmured. "When the man collapsed, it vanished. I didn't see where it went."

I swivelled to my brother. "Did you see?"

"Nope, but I wasn't looking." He didn't look entirely convinced by Jonathan's statements. "I was watching our photographer friend, remember?"

"Speaking of whom, he left through the back door, according to Allie." I caught Jonathan's eye as he attempted to shrink back against the wall. "Did you see anyone taking photos out here?"

"Yes. That's why I'm hiding."

"He has some nerve," I muttered. "Jonathan, do you mind coming back inside? I need to keep tabs on everyone, and Vicky is currently hiding under a pool table while the others are unaccounted for. Do you think the other ghosts saw the same... the same shadow as you did?"

"I didn't see anything," Mart put in. "Why does nobody ever listen to me?"

"I'm listening to you." I watched Jonathan resignedly peel himself away from the wall and then followed him into the inn with my brother at my side. "But if the other ghosts all saw something screwy in the afterworld, it's worth a second look."

"You're not going to tell that ghastly woman *that*, are you?" Mart shuddered.

"Certainly not." She hadn't seen anything awry herself, I was sure, but now I thought back, the man's death had happened so quickly that I hadn't realised my Reaper senses hadn't responded the way they usually did when someone moved into the afterworld.

Weird. Granted, there'd been no reason for me to pay attention to my Reaper senses when my other five senses were perfectly aware of what I'd just witnessed, but if his death *hadn't* been an accident, the only way to confirm either way was to summon his ghost.

There was a lag between the time of death and when a ghost appeared, so I didn't mention my theory to anyone else. Jonathan's ominous pronouncement had officially killed my mood, especially as my attempts to find the rest of the ghosts were futile and Carey didn't come back downstairs throughout the rest of my shift. As a result, I had entirely too much time alone to dwell on the possible reasons my Reaper powers hadn't reacted to the man's death.

My abilities weren't on the fritz again, I was pretty sure. There'd been a brief time a couple of months ago when some of Mina Devlin's cronies had thought it amusing to booby-trap the witches' headquarters and temporarily dampen my Reaper skills, but those witches were in jail, and the coven's new leader wouldn't stand for that sort of nonsense. Not that I could discount the coven's potential involvement in the incident yesterday, given that it would have made Mina Devlin's day to know that our first official ghost tour had ended in disaster.

"I think you're a little paranoid," Mart told me when I mentioned this. "Jia might think everything is the coven's work, but why would they show up on one of our tours? Didn't you vet anyone who signed up?"

"No, that's the problem." Not that anything other than a thorough background check would root out any of Mina Devlin's supporters—and with magic, it was entirely possible for someone to hide their identity. I wasn't that paranoid—or I hadn't been. "Let's face it, Mina's supporters have the most to gain from our downfall."

If anyone would be scheming enough to infiltrate our grand opening and attempt to frame us for murder, it was Mina Devlin, but who among the crowd might have been acting as her agent? How in the world would we ever prove it? Esther alone believed her husband's death to have been anything other than an accident, and I'd sooner take a nude broomstick flight than admit there might have been any truth in her claims.

"Okay, then, how did they commit murder by ghost?" Mart asked. "I'd have thought using poison or a curse would be more their speed."

"It might have been either of those things, just subtler than we planned for." I hadn't seen Esther's husband's body since the paramedics had taken it away, but it was certainly possible to use a potion or curse to mimic a death of natural causes. I'd have to speak to the hospital staff, preferably without being waylaid by the woman herself.

After I weighed the odds, I decided to go to the hospital alone and assess the situation before deciding whether to wade in and talk to anyone. Mart maintained that I was paranoid but didn't decline when I asked if he wanted to come with me, so we set off at the end of my shift.

I hadn't been to the local hospital since before Mina Devlin's departure from town, so I wasn't entirely sure what to expect, but the building itself didn't look any different. The automatic doors slid open to reveal a small waiting room, in which a handful of patients waited. Nobody was at the front desk, which seemed odd.

"Maybe Esther scared off the staff, like Drew said," I whispered to Mart. "Hey—get back here."

He'd drifted down a nearby corridor, and when he ignored my attempts to get his attention, I had no choice but to follow him before I drew too many puzzled looks from the patients. I didn't know which room the body was in, but using my Reaper skills to have a sneaky look around wouldn't lead to anything but trouble.

Already I had second thoughts about my visit here. If I admitted it to myself, I'd hoped to find conclusive proof that

Jonathan was mistaken and that Esther's husband's death had been an accident after all, but the only staff member I was actually familiar with was Cathy, the new coven healer. It was anyone's guess as to how she'd react to seeing me again, given that it was thanks to me that she'd spent time in jail for having helped Mina Devlin cover for some of her numerous crimes. From what I'd seen of her yesterday, I didn't know if she held a grudge. She'd been nothing but professional, but we'd been in public. Meeting her alone had the potential to get ugly. Fast.

I thought of the stark fear on Jonathan's face and the way Vicky had cowered under the table and steeled my nerves before giving my brother a look urging him to stay put. Then I rapped on the door to Cathy's office. Through the gaps around the doorframe, a foul smell emanated from within the room, presumably from whatever potion she was brewing. It smelled like a pair of old hiking boots that had been left out in the rain and only intensified when the door opened.

A familiar frizzy-haired witch with glasses squinted at me from the doorway. "How did I guess you'd come sniffing around here?"

"I'm not sniffing." I was trying to hold my breath, actually, given the stench. "Why did you expect me to show up? Did you speak to Esther?"

"Yes, and she's the reason our receptionist is currently out on leave." She wrinkled her nose. "You don't look like you need a healer, so if you don't mind—"

"I want to talk to the person who examined her husband's body," I said. "Did you verify the cause of death?"

"There hasn't been an autopsy, if that's what you're asking," she said. "These things take time, especially when the next of kin insists upon threatening my fellow staff."

"She did the same to me, so you're not alone there."

She studied my face. "So you came here to cover your tracks, is that it?"

"There's nothing to cover." Also, she was one to talk, having participated in a genuine cover-up herself. "I had nothing to do with his death, but I wanted to verify that magic wasn't involved all the same. Did you see anything on his body that might point to an unusual cause of death?"

"No, I didn't," she replied. "Not that I'm supposed to discuss the subject with the likes of you, Reaper. I notice you've ingratiated yourself with the new coven leader."

"We're acquainted, if that's what you mean." I couldn't figure out her angle. Her grumpiness wasn't anything new, but there didn't seem to be any new layers concealing a simmering grudge over my role in her brief arrest. Might she have retained ties with the ex-coven leader after all, or had she left her past behind her when she'd walked out of jail? "Listen, I know you have no reason to let me in, but if his death did have an unusual cause, then I can help."

"I thought ghosts were your area of expertise, not dead bodies."

"His ghost isn't around." Yet. I fully intended to summon him at the first opportunity, but it was worth checking his body first. "His body is here, and I figured Esther would want it sent home as fast as possible. Can I have a look? I won't touch anything."

"If the police asked, I might say yes," she growled. "You, though? Not a chance."

"You want me to call Drew and ask him to request that you let me visit the morgue?"

"You and Drew are still working together?" Frown lines appeared on her forehead. "Wait. No way. You're a thing?"

To my bewilderment, she burst into laughter, as if I'd told a hilarious joke. Doubled up, she rested a hand on the doorframe, while the smell wafting from the room made my eyes water.

"Have you finished yet?" I said irritably. "This isn't news to anyone else, you know."

"I have a busy schedule. Unlike you, evidently."

"Believe me, I have a dozen things I'd rather be doing than arguing with you," I told her. "I'd like to keep *my* job, which means stopping hysterical widows from sullying our reputation for no good reason. Besides, wouldn't you want to rule out any possible causes of death that she might blame you for not spotting later?"

There was no point in dragging Drew into this when I could use my Reaper abilities to sneak in if Cathy refused to relent, but that didn't mean I wanted to cave in.

"She's welcome to throw around all the blame she likes. It's nothing but hot air." She glowered at me. "You aren't going to let this one slide, are you? Look, there are no signs whatsoever that his death was anything other than an accident."

"I know, but isn't it worth a second look?" I asked. "I don't even have to touch him."

She sighed. "If I say no, I'm going to wake up in the night to you sneaking around the place, aren't I?"

"Do you sleep in here?"

"As a matter of fact, yes," she said. "Believe it or not, I do care about my job, despite your best efforts to whittle my coven down to nothing."

"Several of your fellow coven members kidnapped me and covered up multiple murders." And that wasn't even getting into the coven's involvement in the tragic flood two decades ago. "I know we've had our differences, and I don't want to waste any more of your time, but you saw for yourself that Esther is on a rampage and she's willing to take out anyone in her path. I don't want to give her another reason to come after any of us."

Her eyes narrowed. "One look at the body. *No* touching. That clear?"

"Crystal," I said. "Thanks. Where is the body?"

"In here." She stepped out of the room, bustled down the corridor, and then pushed open another door.

Inside a small room, Jonas's body was laid out on a table. I squinted at him, engaging my Reaper senses, but nothing hit me except for the usual chill of the close presence of the afterworld. No ghosts were present except for my brother, who'd remained outside the room in an unusual act of obedience.

"Happy now?" she asked.

"Not really," I said. "It was definitely a heart attack? You're certain?"

"As far as our tests have shown," she said. "There's magic to consider, too, and for all I know the old hag is right. If she is, I'd rather this was out of our hands, wouldn't you?"

I gave the body one last look and then left the small room, trying to tell myself that I'd have a chance to question his ghost later. Admittedly, the location of a new ghost's appearance tended to vary. Sometimes they showed up at their site of death, but it was just as likely he'd appear at home or another familiar place instead.

Which meant that my best shot at finding his spirit was to summon it directly using my Reaper powers and hope that his angry wife wasn't around to bear witness. No pressure.

5

———

I left the hospital and walked back to the inn, Mart drifting along behind me.

"Stop moping," he said. When I made to protest, he added, "Don't deny it, that's exactly what you're doing."

"I'm thinking," I corrected him. "There's a difference. Don't you think it's weird that my Reaper abilities didn't kick in when Jonas died?"

"They didn't?"

"Not that I'm aware of." I extended a hand and summoned the shadows of the afterworld, watching the darkness swirl around my palm. "At least they seem to be in working order."

"You thought the witches pranked you again?"

"Wouldn't be the first time." If I pursued my theory of the coven's involvement in Jonas's death, then maybe I ought to have asked Cathy more questions, but I was already lucky that she hadn't simply slammed the door in my face. Besides, even if this *was* the coven's doing, then there was no proof anyone in the local community had been their instrument. At least half the people on the tour yesterday had been from outside of Hawkwood Hollow, and considering Mina Devlin was no longer living in the town, there was the undeniable possibility that she'd acquired new allies since her absence.

The one person who might know why my abilities hadn't reacted was the local Reaper, but he was a recluse, and every visit I paid to his house ended in me leaving in frustration without any answers. No, I'd save that option for last and try to find the other ghosts first, and I'd see if any of them backed up Jonathan's observations.

When I walked into the restaurant, Carey came running over to me, her expression distraught. "Maura, where have you been? Have you seen this?"

She beckoned me to a table, on which she'd set up her laptop. The screen showed a large photo of the inn displayed under the heading, "New Ghost Tour Business Dead and Buried." Carey scrolled down the article, which contained another photo, this one of the paramedics and the police clustered around Esther's husband's body. I didn't need to look for the author's name to guess the culprit was Parker Maven. Oh hell.

"That guy." My hands curled into fists. "I'm sorry, Carey. I provoked him into doing this."

"He's right, though," she said tremulously. "Nothing he said in the article was a lie, and now everyone who follows his blog will know that Esther wants to shut us down."

"How would he know that?" Had he been eavesdropping earlier when I'd been talking to Allie? He had some cheek, sneaking around taking pictures and listening in on our conversations and then acting as if he had the moral high ground. "He's just playing for attention, Carey. Don't let him get to you."

"People *are* paying attention," she said. "His post already has a thousand hits. We're finished."

"That's not true." Allie would be much better at reassuring her than I was, but when I peered through the doorway to the reception area, I saw her talking on the phone to someone. *Please don't say Esther is pestering her again.*

Carey caught me looking. "My mum won't tell me everything, but I know some people have cancelled their bookings for the next tour."

"Not everyone," I said. "Seriously, Jia will be here tomorrow, and she'll help us come up with a plan of action. That guy shouldn't have been allowed to take photos of the property in the first place, especially when the emergency services were here."

"But he did." She lowered her gaze. "The article said my mum might be prosecuted and that Esther was seeking legal action."

"He doesn't know anything, Carey," I told her. "Really, don't give him another minute of your time. We'll have a movie night this evening. That'll cheer you up. Right, Mart?"

I looked for my brother and saw that he'd vanished, presumably to seek out his fellow ghosts in the games room. After making sure Carey had closed down the web page showing Parker's blog, I followed him.

Pulling my phone out of my pocket, I loaded up the website—*Dead Serious*, the blog was called—and then entered the games room. A pool cue swung around and nearly hit me in the eye, and I swatted it away. "Hey!"

"Sorry." Jonathan sheepishly dropped the pool cue back onto the table. "We were about to start a game."

"We have a crisis." I lifted my phone to display the article. "Mart, are you paying attention?"

He pulled a face at me. "Can't you see we're busy here?"

"Look—if you want either of us to have a job by the end of the week, then I need you to help me figure out what to do about this."

I showed him my phone screen, and he gave it a rude gesture. "Yes, I know our delightful blogger is spewing hot air everywhere. Since when was that news?"

"It's worse than we expected." From my brief skim of the article, he'd posted pictures of the inn from pretty much every angle as well as insulting everyone who worked here, ghosts included. "According to Carey, his blog's really popular with the online ghost-tour community. Not only is he bad-mouthing our business, but he somehow found out that Esther wants to pursue legal action against us."

"Why?" Jonathan blanched, and behind him, I saw Vicky shrink back in her seat on the sofa. "Because her husband's death wasn't an accident?"

"Because she's paranoid," I said firmly. "I know what you saw, Jonathan, but I went to the hospital and checked his body, and it looks completely normal. Not that I don't believe you, but we shouldn't be publicising this when Esther is already convinced we're responsible for his death. If we take the blame, we'll all get arrested."

"I can go and haunt her," Mart suggested. "That might shut her up."

"If anything, it'd do the opposite," I said. "No haunting. We need to cheer Carey up, though. Also, Drew's coming over in a bit."

"And I'm supposed to be excited about that... why?"

"You still get to pick the movie for tonight, remember?"

"I thought it was my turn," said Jonathan.

"I promised Mart in exchange for a favour," I said to him. "You can decide next week instead. Have either of you seen any of the other ghosts yet?"

"Nope," said Mart. "They're lying low, I expect."

"I'll have another look." Mart and I had checked the upstairs rooms earlier, but we were bound to have missed a few possible hiding spots. When we found them, the best-case scenario was that the other ghosts refuted Jonathan's suspicion about Jonas's death and confirmed he'd been mistaken, but that was wishful thinking on my part.

I left the room and made for the stairs to the upper floor, mentally running through the places I hadn't searched yet. The fire escape was a starting point, so I opened the heavy door and almost collided with a bespectacled witch with curly brown hair. She took a startled step back, a pen tucked behind her glasses and a clipboard underneath one arm. "Ah —sorry, I got lost."

"The stairs are that way." I pointed behind me. "That's the fire door."

The sign ought to have given her a clue, but I'd already ticked off one guest and I didn't need to give anyone else a negative impression, even a trespasser.

"Oh." A flush covered her freckled cheeks. "You're Maura, right?"

"That's me." I was pretty sure she'd been on yesterday's tour, but I wasn't otherwise familiar with her. "You?"

"Sofia Granger."

As she edged around me, my gaze caught on the clipboard in her hand. "Hey—isn't that one of ours?"

"This?" She held up the clipboard. "I borrowed it. I hope you don't mind."

I hoped she'd asked Carey or Allie's permission, considering Carey had been using that clipboard during yesterday's tour. "You were on the ghost tour yesterday?"

"I was, yes," she said. "You have an interesting approach. I've been taking notes all day."

"For what reason?" I queried. "Are you a reviewer?"

"Oh, not a professional one," she said. "I'm setting up something similar to your business myself, so I'm doing a kind of unofficial tour of all the haunted attractions around this part of the country. Checking out the competition and distinguishing the fakes from the real deal."

That was news to me. "Can you see ghosts?"

I'd surely know if she could, but her words rubbed me up the wrong way. Was that why she'd been lurking behind the fire door? Had she been looking for proof that we'd been faking?

"No, but you can," she said. "Is it true that you're a Reaper?"

Where had she heard that? If a local had told her, then it'd be hard to refute, but I didn't need word spreading to other people who'd been on the tour too. Esther and Parker had already left the inn, but if anyone else here was in contact with them, then I'd land in a sticky situation. *All right, I'll give her the benefit of the doubt.*

"Half," I answered. "I'm not an official Reaper. I work for the inn."

She gave a nod, a pleased smile on her face. "Yes, that makes sense. I did wonder why the Reapers would let one of their own people run ghost tours. It seems to run counter to their secrecy laws."

Luckily for both of us, my phone buzzed, affording me the excuse to walk away from her questions. When I saw Drew was calling me, I returned to the stairs to answer. "Hey, Drew. Are you on your way?"

"Sure, I'm five minutes away. I heard you were at the hospital earlier…"

I groaned under my breath. "Sorry. I should probably have told you first, but I didn't want to bother you at work."

"You didn't go to look at Jonas's body?" Concern laced his voice. "Did you?"

"I looked, but I didn't touch anything," I said ineffectually. "Don't worry, I asked Cathy for permission. She wasn't thrilled to see me, but she's as keen to get rid of Esther as the rest of us are."

"Then why did you go to look at his body in the first place?"

"I'll tell you when you're here." No need to risk any potential eavesdroppers getting any ideas when Parker had decided to put us on public blast and now this Sofia had set herself up as a rival. Maybe I should have background-screened all our guests before they'd shown up for the tour, but that was a level of paranoia worthy of Mina Devlin herself.

True to his word, Drew showed up five minutes later. I told him about Jonathan's claims, adding that I wanted to keep Carey from finding out as long as humanly possible. She had enough to worry about, between Esther's complaints and Parker's public condemnation—not to mention Sofia's scheming. While Drew and I joined Carey and her mother in the restaurant for dinner, I asked if they were aware that a guest had borrowed one of their clipboards.

"Certainly not," Allie answered. "Sofia Granger? I think I remember her."

"Yeah." I glanced at Carey, who'd calmed down somewhat following her unwelcome discovery of Parker's article. "I found her lurking in a fire escape. She claimed to be researching so she can set up a tour company of her own."

"That's all we need." Carey dropped her fork. "What if she comes up with a copy of one of our tours and then has a successful launch *without* anyone dying in the middle of the first tour? Then nobody will ever book with us again."

"She can't copy every part of our tour when she doesn't have our ghosts," Allie reminded her.

"Exactly," I said. "I'll talk to her. She needs to give that clipboard back before she leaves."

I'd sooner have dived into one of Cathy's foul-smelling cauldrons than attempted a friendly chat with her after our last encounter, but someone had to do it.

Carey slumped back in her seat. "First Parker tells everyone we killed someone and now this."

"There must be something we can do to challenge him." I looked to Allie, then Drew, who shook his head.

"He hasn't done anything illegal," Drew said. "As for the photos he posted… well, the person who has the most reason to object is Esther, since it was her husband whose body was in the photos."

My hands clenched on the table. "Yeah, it's disrespectful, to say the least, but I'm not sure she's seen the article yet. Either way, I think it's safe to say that Parker doesn't care about that guy's death. All he wants is to make us look bad."

"And he succeeded." Carey's eyes brimmed over with tears again. "I don't want you to lie to me. I know this is bad news. I don't know what I'll say at school on Monday if someone brings it up."

"Wait—" But she was already on her feet and walking away. As she left the restaurant, I groaned. "Sorry. I shouldn't have mentioned him again."

"It wasn't just you," said Allie. "She needs a decent night's sleep if you ask me. Poor thing."

"So do I," I said. "We'll do a low-key movie night, since we only have three ghosts around at the moment."

Allie's brows shot up. "Wait, the ghosts are gone?"

"Don't tell Carey," I said hastily. "They went into hiding after that guy died, but they're still around. I managed to track down two of them, and Jia can help me find the others."

"I hope you're right." Allie went to follow her daughter, while I rested my head in the palm of my hand.

"She was already upset," said Drew. "It's not your fault."

"I'm partly responsible for kicking off Parker's grudge," I said. "He was being unbearable *before* Jonas died, but the size of his platform is going to be a problem if he keeps sharing that Esther is actually trying to pursue legal action against us. I don't know how he even found out, to be honest."

"It looks more as if he's playing for attention," he said. "Stirring up controversy without any proof. It's hard to ignore something like that, I know, but for Carey's sake…"

"Yeah, I'm not telling her I went to the hospital."

"Why *did* you go?" He studied my face. "You didn't think Esther might be correct about her husband's death, did you?"

"No, but one of the ghosts… well, he claimed he saw a weird shadow when Jonas dropped dead. I wanted to check out his body to see if anything was amiss."

"Weird how?" asked Drew.

"I don't know, but when a ghost says it's weird, I take notice," I said. "I didn't find any clues at the hospital, so I'm going to wait and summon Jonas's ghost and ask if *he* saw any weird shadows."

"Maura."

"Drew." I met his stern look with one of equal defiance. "Don't fight me on this one. It's our business at stake, remember?"

"That's precisely why you need to tread carefully with Esther—and summoning her husband's ghost definitely does not fall into that category," he said. "Is this ghost of yours trustworthy?"

"Yes, and I know for a fact that none of our ghosts were anywhere near Jonas or his wife when he died," I said. "They can sometimes see things regular people can't, though, which is why I was inclined to take a second look at Jonas's body. Also, there's another thing… my Reaper powers didn't react to his death."

"You didn't mention that earlier."

"That would be because I didn't notice." I rubbed my forehead with my knuckles. "I saw him die, so it's not as if I'd have needed any reaction from my Reaper powers to clue me in. I'm not sure why they didn't react, but I figured that we're better off staying a step or two ahead of Esther, so I wanted to make sure her claims didn't have any truth to them. It's fortunate that *she* can't see ghosts, or else she'd be pointing fingers directly at our employees and not just Allie."

"Does she know ghosts can't be arrested?"

"Honestly, I'm not sure that would matter," I replied. "Not when she's on a crusade. Anyway, it wasn't a ghost Jonathan saw. They don't cast shadows."

Assuming he was right, there were plenty of magical reasons a man might randomly drop dead of apparent natural causes, ranging from complex curses to deadly beasts from the depths of the afterworld. If the latter, I could only hope that I'd had a lapse in attention and not that something had evaded my Reaper senses.

"Be careful, Maura," Drew said. "I know you're going to stand your ground, but this case has the potential to make our lives difficult in multiple ways, and if Esther gets wind of your suspicions…"

"She's incapable of listening to any voice that isn't her own," I said. "I'm not going to drop any hints in front of her, don't worry. I just figured it was worth taking all the options into consideration in case they come back to hit us later."

"I'll listen out for any new rumours," said Drew. "My department already has their hands full, so if Esther expects us to take her claims seriously without any basis, then she'll be waiting awhile."

"Good," I said. "I hope she doesn't see Parker's review in the meantime."

"Should I go and haunt him?" Mart came drifting over to our table and tried unsuccessfully to pick up the fork from beside Carey's abandoned plate. "I can *persuade* him to take down that post of his."

"I highly doubt that would improve the situation." To Drew, I added, "Mart thinks Parker deserves a haunting."

"He does," said Mart. "He didn't even mention me in his review."

"He can't *see* you." Man, I was tired. "I'm within my rights to send him an email asking him to take down those photos out of respect for the dead, but I bet he'd laugh at me."

"You can try anyway," Drew said. "Isn't there an email address or contact form on his blog? It's not as if you're being unreasonable by asking."

"Exactly," said Mart. "I can help you craft an email—or better, I can write it for you."

"Definitely not," I said. "I'll write it myself—not you, Mart."

He pouted. "Why not?"

"If the email consists of a string of four-letter words, it's not going to improve the situation."

"Spoilsport."

Still, there might be something to the idea of opening up a dialogue between the inn and Parker Maven. With Allie's permission.

When she returned to the restaurant, I went to ask her. "Hey, Allie. Is it okay if I email Parker tomorrow and ask him to take down those photos of Jonas's body?"

"Are you sure?"

"Positive," I said. "I'm not the inn's owner, so he can threaten me all he likes and it won't matter."

"Well… all right," Allie said. "Stick to a simple polite email."

Parker hadn't exactly been polite, but I didn't want to cause any more trouble than I already had. "I will. Where's Carey?"

"She's in bed," she said. "She needs the rest, given that she hardly slept last night."

Neither had I, but I had an email to craft before I could sleep. I didn't believe for an instant that Parker would respond to reasonable demands, but it gave me a productive line of action to take while I waited to question Jonas's ghost.

6

The following morning brought a suspicious absence of unwelcome news, though with it being Sunday, the universe might have taken the day off. Since Drew had stayed overnight, I waited until after he left to send the message I'd composed to Parker the previous night.

When I went downstairs to find the others, Allie was at her usual spot behind the front desk, but Carey was nowhere to be seen.

"She's okay. She's just catching up on schoolwork," Allie said in explanation. "I know she's dreading tomorrow."

I grimaced. "Can't you ask her teachers not to bring up the subject?"

"I can try, but you know what kids are like," she said. "Anyway, did you send that email?"

"To Parker?" I asked. "Yeah, I did. Not sure it'll be of any help, but it was worth a shot."

"I know." She rubbed her tired eyes. "I have to admit Esther's getting under my skin more than I like. I know I keep telling Carey that her threats will come to nothing, but

I'm getting concerned that she might actually press charges against us."

"For what?" I asked. "You didn't endanger her husband's life. He willingly walked in here wanting to be scared by ghosts, so if she wants to make us sound irresponsible, then she's going to have a hard time."

"She can certainly try." She yawned. "I was up half the night running internet searches on similar situations, but most of them didn't involve real ghosts, just hoaxes."

"People died on fake ghost tours?" I gave an eye roll. "See, there's no limit to the ways people can get themselves killed in ridiculous situations. If a roof tile had fallen on his head, would she have tried to arrest the roof?"

Allie managed a weak smile. "No, but don't forget we have a responsibility for the safety of the guests."

"We also have dozens of witnesses who saw her husband's death was an accident."

Granted, at least two of them had a reason to want our business to fail and the rest might be hard to reach, but Esther's lack of actual evidence would be her downfall. I hoped.

"We'll see what happens next week," she said. "Jia should be here soon, right?"

"Yes, so we can find those missing ghosts." No doubt they were hiding in distant corners, not wanting to be disturbed. Jia would help me think of places I hadn't searched yet, and if all else failed, I could use my Reaper abilities to unearth them. "I'm going to get breakfast."

Jia showed up as I was in the process of swiping some coffee from the buffet table. "Hey, Maura. Did you see that blog post?"

"You mean on Parker's blog?" Suspicion rose. "There wasn't another one, was there?"

"Not to my knowledge," she said. "What a nasty piece of

work that guy is, though. The things he said about us were bad enough, but those photos… well, I actually sent him an email asking what the hell he was playing at."

"You didn't, did you?" I pressed a hand to my forehead. "I did too. Now he's going to think we're harassing him."

"Oh no. I should have asked you first." She swore under her breath. "Sorry, I got all wound up when I thought of how awful Carey must feel."

"Yeah, she's having a rough time of it," I said. "She even skipped out on the movie night yesterday and has spent most of the past day hiding in her room."

"I wish I'd been here. My date was a no-show." She helped herself to a coffee, too, and joined me behind the bar.

"If it isn't my favourite living person." Mart popped up behind us with a twirl.

"Excuse me?" I feigned an insulted tone. "I'm the one who brought you back from the dead, in case you've forgotten."

"That's more of a benefit to you than to me, because I'm too awesome for the afterworld," said Mart.

"Sure you are."

Jia grinned. "Where are the others, anyway?"

"The other ghosts?" I asked. "Well, Vicky and Jonathan are hiding in the games room, and I don't know where the others are. They've been missing since the tour on Friday."

"Seriously?"

"Yeah, I'm actually starting to worry about them." I dropped my voice, though there were few people around this early on a Sunday. "I know I can use my abilities to find them even if they're on the other side of town, but I don't need to freak them out any more than they already are."

"Speaking of the afterworld, have you seen Jonas's ghost yet?"

"Not yet, no," I said. "You know there's usually a delay, but if he's going to show up, it's probably going to be today or tomorrow. If he doesn't appear at the inn, I'm going to try summoning him."

"Erm... why?" she asked. "I was only being half-serious, you know. Unless—wait, you don't think his death wasn't an accident... do you?"

"Don't spread that around," I said in a low voice, "but Jonathan insisted he saw something weird when the guy died."

I relayed our discussion from the previous day, adding in a mention of my visit to the hospital.

Jia shook her head at me. "I'm surprised Cathy didn't slam the door on you."

"She actually did let me look at the body, for all the use it was," I said. "It's worth a talk with Jonas's ghost to cover our bases."

"I suppose," she said. "Not that it'll be much help with staving off his widow, though. We don't want *her* getting wind of this."

"Exactly," I said. "The other weird thing is that my Reaper skills didn't alert me to his death. I'm not sure why."

"They didn't?" Her brow wrinkled. "Did you ask the Reaper? I know he's not the type to offer help..."

"No, which is why I want to see if the other ghosts back up Jonathan's word before I go and poke that particular bear."

We started our ghost search on the lower floor of the inn and then made for the stairs, where I seized the chance to search the fire escape in case Sofia was lurking inside again. We found nobody, though, living or dead. After finishing up our search, the two of us returned to the lobby in defeat.

"I think it's going to be easier if you do this the Reaper way, Maura," said Jia. "You can try summoning Jonas afterwards too. That way you'll kill two birds with one stone. Or four ghosts."

"Hey!" Mart protested. "I object to that."

"You're already dead, stop being oversensitive." Jia turned to me. "Want to do it in here or outside?"

"Outside. We don't need to freak out any potential customers." While the inn might advertise itself as a haunted establishment, that didn't mean people would be anything other than horrified at seeing the genuine afterlife appear in the lobby.

I made for the backyard before I summoned the shadows of the afterworld to my hands. As darkness swept in around me, Jia kept her distance and ducked back into the inn. I didn't blame her. She might be able to see ghosts, but the sight of the void that awaited on the other side of the grave was enough to strike fear into anyone who wasn't a Reaper.

"Louise?" I called into the darkness. "Wade? Brian?"

No answer came, at least not at first. Then after a long pause, Wade came shuffling into view, eyes widening at the sight of the darkness surrounding him. "What is this?"

"The afterworld. I had to use my Reaper powers to find you," I said. "Seriously, where were you hiding?"

"Upstairs," he mumbled. "Why'd you want to talk to me?"

"Because you and all the other ghosts disappeared on Friday night and freaked Maura out," Mart answered for me.

"That's not it, Mart." I stepped into my brother's path to talk to the other ghost. "We can't run a haunted inn without ghosts, can we?"

"I thought we weren't running any more tours," Wade said.

"Why does everyone keep saying that?" I said, irritated. "The incident on Friday was unfortunate, yes, but Jonas's death was an accident, according to everyone who examined the body. So unless we find evidence to the contrary—"

"They're wrong," mumbled the middle-aged ghost.

My gaze snapped upwards. "What?"

From behind the patch of darkness, Jia reappeared. "Wade, what do you mean by that? How was his death not an accident?"

"A ghost killed him." A feminine voice spoke, making Jia jump and disappear from view again, but it was only Louise. The older woman emerged from the shadows at Wade's side, her expression as serious as his own. "I thought you knew."

"What?" I looked between them. "You think a *ghost* killed Jonas? Which ghost?"

"I don't know," said Louise. "I only caught a glimpse."

"Jonathan said he saw a shadow..." I trailed off. "I also looked at Jonas's body, though, and there were no signs to indicate his death was anything other than an accident."

"Did you really see a ghost?" Jia stepped forwards again. "If you did, it would help if you gave us a description."

"I wasn't looking directly at—at the victim," said Louise. "Not until he died, and then I saw... movement, in the after-world. I can't describe it, since everything is so dark over there, but yes... it looked like a shadow."

"I believe you, but if there really was a ghost involved with his death, it definitely wasn't one of our employees." That much was clear. "And this mystery ghost isn't at the inn. Believe me, I searched every corner while I was trying to find you."

"That doesn't mean it's safe," Wade insisted. "The ghost might come back."

"If it does, I'll send it packing myself." When neither of them appeared convinced, I looked to Jia for backup. "What else can I do? It's not like I can put sage around the inn without driving off our ghostly employees."

Besides, if a ghost had genuinely killed Jonas, then why would it have stayed at the scene of the crime? Jonas hadn't been local, and it shouldn't be our problem if he'd somehow attracted the wrath of a vengeful spirit.

"Come back into the inn," Jia told the two ghosts. "There's no danger here to anyone, and Vicky and Jonathan are waiting for you in the games room. Where's Brian, do you know?"

"Oh, he left," Wade said. "Went back to his old haunt."

"What?" I'd forgotten that Jia had initially brought Brian to the inn from the other side of town. "You can find him, can't you?"

"Yes, but if he won't answer through the afterworld, I'd say he wants to be left alone." For the first time in a long while, Jia appeared genuinely spooked.

"He's an employee, though," I said. "We need him back before Tuesday's tour."

"That's still going ahead?"

"Don't you start too." I sighed. "Why does everyone keep assuming we're going to stop running ghost tours?"

"Because we're possibly getting sued for causing some-one's death and we also got bad-mouthed across the entire online ghost blogger community?" Jia queried.

"The talk will only get worse if we let it affect our busi-ness," I said. "Besides, if you look at the other reviews, they're almost all glowing."

"Yeah, but I expected Carey to want to put the tours on hiatus," said Jia. "Have you asked?"

"No, but having to cancel wouldn't improve her mood," I said. "Parker isn't the entirety of the online ghost blogging community. This'll blow over."

"I hope you're right," she said. "If Carey wants to carry on running the tours, I'm game."

"Good." I turned back to the dark expanse of the after-world and called for our last missing ghost. "Brian? Are you in there?"

Wade and Louise drifted out of my line of sight, but Brian didn't materialise from the gloom.

"I'll go to his old haunt and find him," Jia offered. "Are you going to summon Jonas's ghost next?"

"Not here!" Louise blanched. "What if his killer comes back too?"

"I highly doubt it." When both she and Wade gave me a pointed stare, I relented and let the shadows fade away. "Fine, I'll go somewhere else if you two go back into the inn. Deal?"

They obeyed, while Jia and I entered behind them. The restaurant remained empty of customers, so I had time for another ghost-summoning session before we started work.

"Honestly, you'd think they didn't *live* in the afterworld," I remarked to Jia. "Well, not *live*, but you know what I mean."

"Yeah… it takes a lot to freak out a ghost, though," she said. "A ghost murdering a human has got to be surreal to witness, even from the afterworld."

"If they're right, it can't possibly be a regular ghost." I'd need to dig into my rusty memories of my Reaper training to pursue that line of thought. Most spirits couldn't touch living people, and if by all outside appearances Jonas had appeared to have had a heart attack, then any proof was on shaky ground. Which was good news for our defence against Esther's complaints, but bad news for finding the killer.

And if Esther turned out to have been right, then the other ghosts had a reason to be scared that had nothing to do with any invisible killers lurking in the afterworld.

After the ghosts had retreated to the games room, Jia and I walked around to the front of the inn. While she went in search of Brian, I headed to a spot I'd unofficially chosen as the ideal site for summoning ghosts, where a large tree blocked anyone from the inn from seeing the darkness that swathed my hands.

I spoke Jonas's name, but no response came.

"Jonas Wrigley," I repeated, and again. "Jonas?"

"Guess he moved on," Mart commented from behind me. "No big loss."

"His wife would beg to differ." I let the shadows fade away and returned to the restaurant to start my shift. "Where is everyone?"

"Sleeping in." Mart did a tap dance on one of the empty tables. "It's boring in here."

"Then go and watch the other ghosts," I told him. "Make sure nobody pulls a disappearing act again."

Carey had yet to emerge from her room, so I paced alone behind the bar while I waited for Jia to return. Since the other ghosts were confined to the games room, I tried yet again to contact Jonas's spirit and was met with nothing but shadows.

That left me with one remaining option… the non-Reaper method of summoning a ghost.

"I'm almost out of herbs for summoning," I said to Jia when she finally returned with a subdued Brian in tow. "I should have grabbed some while I was at the hospital."

"I still can't believe you went there." She bounded behind the bar to join me. "And that you spoke to Cathy of all people. I'm surprised she didn't hex you."

"Yeah." I yawned. "Did you know one another?"

"No, but we're the same age, so we met a few times," she said. "I remember her being moody when she was an apprentice, but not one of Mina's cronies."

I pulled a face. "All she did was help cover up a few murders and get the job as her coven healer."

"You'll be hard-pressed to find a coven member who didn't help Mina in some way, intentionally or not," she said. "Not that I'm defending her, mind. Is it just me or is it weirdly quiet in here?"

"It is." Not that unusual for a Sunday, but I had to wonder

if word had begun to spread of Esther's comments. Or worse... Parker's. "Yesterday was fine."

"And we still have plenty of bookings for next week." Jia's tone suggested that she wanted to reassure herself as well as me.

"We should ask Allie how many people did end up booking onto the next tour," I added. "Oh, and I need to ask that Sofia to give that clipboard back."

"Wait, who?"

"Sofia Granger," I clarified. "She was on Friday's tour and is still here because she's supposedly setting up her own ghost-tour business. She also borrowed Carey's clipboard without asking, so we're not exactly best friends."

"I know that name." Jia's forehead scrunched up. "Sofia... she used to be in the coven."

"She did?"

"Yeah, but I didn't recognise her on the tour... which isn't that odd given that I haven't seen her in a decade."

"Well, she's staying at the inn." I glanced over at the door connecting the restaurant to the lobby, in case she was lurking out of sight again. "She was in the coven?"

"Yeah, until she left town." A frown pulled at her mouth. "She's planning to run ghost tours? Really?"

"Yeah, she seemed to be checking out the competition."

"Weird." Her jaw twitched. "I swear she said she was never coming back to town. Granted, I did, too, but I'm curious as to why she changed her mind."

"Now I am too." Suspicion rose inside me. "You know, the coven has a good reason to want to sink our tour business, and I wondered if they might have expanded their recruitment base. Not that I want to start a fight with another guest, but if you think she might be worth talking to..."

"Good point," she said. "Bringing an angry ghost to

commit murder sounds exactly like the coven's kind of thing."

"What ghost?" Mart came zipping over to us, rattling the glasses on the bar. "Who?"

"I thought you were watching the other ghosts." I gave him a pointed look.

"They're all doom and gloom in there," he said. "Figured out who our mysterious ghostly killer is yet?"

"No, but we do have a potential suspect," Jia said. "Sofia, an ex-coven member."

"Really," I said, when Mart scoffed in disbelief. "You know it makes perfect sense for Mina to have recruited ex-members who left town, and it might be worth questioning her while she's here at the inn."

"She's here?" Mart asked. "If you need a reason to get her out of her room, I can flood the shower. Just let me know which room it is, and I'll do it."

"Definitely not." If she turned out to be innocent, then Mart's antics would only knock our reputation down a further notch. "Though… I can claim to be looking for a ghost and ask to search her room. It's almost true, and it's not like she can see them."

"True," said Jia. "While we're up there, we can persuade Carey to come out of her room too."

"I think she's worried about school tomorrow. Those kids can be brutal enough without adding another reason for them to bully her."

"Then we'll talk to her." She led the way out of the restaurant into the lobby, and I followed, waving at Allie behind the desk.

"I know there aren't any customers, don't worry," she said before I could speak. "Did you find all the ghosts?"

"Yeah, we did," Jia told her. "I rounded everyone up."

"Something scared them, didn't it?" Allie's shrewdness

made me blink in surprise. "Something other than Jonas's death, I mean."

"Yes." I might as well be honest with her. "I'm not sure what it was, but I'm trying to find out."

"You don't know?" Concern flickered in her eyes. "That… that's a little concerning."

You have no idea.

"Yeah… we're off to talk to Sofia, since she turned out to be an ex-coven member," I said. "I can ask her for your clipboard back while we're at it. Which room is she in?"

Allie scanned the computer screen in front of her. "She's in number fifteen. Are you sure she's from the coven?"

"She left years ago, but I thought it was worth talking to her," I said. "Especially as she's a potential rival."

It was time to see what Sofia had to say for herself.

7

J ia and I made for the stairs, while Mart zipped ahead of us in barely concealed glee at the prospect of getting to make mischief. When we reached room number fifteen, he floated straight through the door before Jia and I had the chance to knock.

Sofia opened the door a moment later, regarding me with a frown. "Can I help you?"

"We're looking for a ghost," I told her, as a box of makeup slid off the desk with a clatter. "Erm. That ghost."

Sofia glanced over her shoulder, her gaze travelling straight through Mart, before turning her attention back to me—and Jia. Upon seeing the latter, her eyes widened with recognition.

"Hi," said Jia. "Fancy meeting you here."

"Jia?" Sofia said. "I thought you weren't coming back."

"You said the same yourself," Jia said. "I came back because I was offered a job, and since I'm no longer in the coven, I don't have to deal with their drama. You?"

"I'm not here permanently," she said. "I just came to check out the inn."

Tension rippled in the air, though Mart continued to cavort around in the background behind Sofia, knocking things over. It was a tad distracting to say the least.

"Yeah, Maura said you're here to research the local ghost-tour companies," said Jia. "I didn't know you were interested in that sort of thing."

"Sure, I saw an online ad for your place and couldn't resist coming back to my old haunts," said Sofia. "This town is just as dreary as I remember, but I understand why you wanted to try to revive its tourist scene. Pity it turned out the way it did."

A muscle ticked in Jia's jaw, while I wondered if Sofia was aware of how rude she was being. Likely yes, but I did want to know if she'd played a role in the mayhem the other night. If she couldn't see Mart, then it was a stretch to imagine her summoning a lethal ghost on the property, let alone bringing one with her. Few ghosts were mobile enough to trail after a living person.

Mart, the only exception I knew, continued to dance above her desk in unrestrained glee. He'd have easily spotted any signs of dodgy magic in her room, so I could only assume nothing was amiss.

"Yes, it's a pity," I said, "but our next tour is scheduled to go ahead as planned, and we don't expect any more derailments."

"Really?" Her brows rose. "I'm surprised, given the negative press you're getting online, but it's your choice, of course."

Oh boy. Of course she would have seen Parker's review, if she was engaged in the online ghost blogger community, but had she played a part in spreading that negative press herself? I didn't know.

"Parker Maven's blog doesn't represent the entirety of the

population of the magical world with an interest in ghosts," I told her. "Not everyone lives online."

"Well, good luck," she said. "Have you found your ghost?"

"Yes." I beckoned to Mart, who was pulling ridiculous faces in the mirror at his non-existent reflection. "Can I have our clipboard back now too?"

"Oh, right." She ducked back into the room and darted over to the desk, picking up the clipboard. In another bound, she pushed it into my hand. "There you go."

"Thanks." I wanted to take her to task for "borrowing" it without permission in the first place, but she closed the door before Jia or I could speak another word.

Mart blew a raspberry at the closed door, and I beckoned him to follow me out of hearing distance before asking, "Did you see any signs that she's been summoning ghosts of her own?"

"No," he said. "Did you really think she'd have dared to try it in her room?"

"It's more likely that she summoned it in town than brought it with her." Spirits were notoriously hard to control, even for the likes of me. Mart, whose existence was literally tethered to mine, did whatever he liked most of the time. What chance would a non-Reaper stand? "Maybe we should have asked if she's seen any of the coven members lately. One of them might have given her a hand."

"I doubt she'd admit it if she did," Jia said sourly. "She wasn't in deeply in Mina Devlin's circle when I knew her, but she was always rude and snotty to anyone she viewed as not in her league. We left the coven around the same time, I think."

"Hmm."

Sofia hadn't acknowledged Jia while she'd been on the tour itself, either, though she hadn't appeared to recognise her until we'd gone to her door.

Jia eyed the clipboard in my hands. "I don't *think* she's likely to have been involved in what happened on Friday, but I'd rather not have her on our next tour."

"She can't be staying here that long, surely," I said. "She hasn't booked a ticket for the next one, as far as I know."

Though it was anyone's guess as to how many people would actually show up, given today's lack of customers in the restaurant.

"Nope," said Jia. "Right. It's time to get Carey out of her room."

"Sounds like a plan," I said. "I can head to the coven's headquarters and grab some more supplies to try summoning Jonas's ghost and ask if any of them is acquainted with Sofia while I'm at it."

"Good call," she said. "Want me to come with you?"

I thought. "Nah, you talk Carey into coming downstairs, since you're more likely to be able to persuade her than I am. I'll go by myself."

The coven leader wouldn't be in her office on Sunday, so I'd be able to slip in and out of their headquarters without anyone else realising I was there. Yes, I was theoretically allowed to come and go as I pleased, but that didn't mean I wanted the coven to figure out what I wanted the herbs for. Namely, finding Jonas's ghost.

Especially if any of their ex-members had been involved in his death.

———

The following morning brought two pieces of unwelcome news. While I'd managed to get my hands on the supplies from the coven's headquarters the previous day without any hitches, I'd opted to wait until Carey wasn't around to try a proper summoning spell. After Jia had finally coaxed Carey out of her room, I hadn't wanted to ruin the mood by alluding to my suspicions regarding Jonas's death.

When Carey left for school on Monday morning, I left Jia temporarily in charge of dealing with customers while I walked to our designated ghost-summoning spot near the river. As I neared the bridge, I caught sight of Carey's distant figure on the other side of the fast-flowing water, easily recognisable by her mustard-yellow uniform and bright-red ghost goggles. I knew she was putting on a brave face, but she had to be petrified of facing her classmates, and it made me doubly determined to figure out what was going on before she ended up having to shoulder the blame for the whole catastrophe.

Which started with finding our elusive ghost.

I set up the concoction of herbs I'd snagged from the coven in a circle and then summoned the shadows of the afterworld to my hands for good measure. I didn't know if the latter actually made a difference, but if this was my last shot to reach Jonas's ghost, I'd make it count.

"Jonas," I said into the circle. "Jonas Wrigley."

No response came. I tried every variation of a summoning command possible before kicking the remnants of the herbs into the river to avoid anyone else using them. Defeated, I returned to the inn.

Jia met me at the door. "No luck?"

"Nope," I grumbled. Then I caught sight of her grim expression. "Wait... what is it?"

"Well." She drew in a breath. "I may have got a reply from a certain blogger."

"Parker actually replied?"

"Not directly." She drew in a breath. "You might want to have a look on his blog."

"He can't have posted another review. What else is there to say?"

"More of an update than a review. Not a nice one either."

Steeling myself, I pulled out my phone and loaded up Parker's blog as I joined Jia behind the bar. Sure enough, Parker had updated his review with a few choice comments directed at the pair of us.

"He says we tried to intimidate him into taking down his post?" I read. "Seriously? He didn't even reply to our emails or try to have a conversation."

"I know, right?" Jia said irritably. "Because we didn't contact him publicly, the people who read his blog won't know any better."

"I still can't believe anyone reads that drivel, personally." I tapped on the contact form on his blog and was met with an error message when I put in my email address. "Wait... has he blocked me from emailing him?"

"Oh, how mature." She tapped at her own phone screen. "He did the same to me. Do you want to post a public comment or should I?"

"Sure, go ahead." We didn't have much to lose at this point. "Mention you have screenshots of the original email conversation saved as proof if necessary."

"Believe me, I kept records." Jia began tapping furiously on the screen while I watched the door for any potential customers. Yesterday we'd had a few people trickle in eventually, but the restaurant still seemed much quieter than usual. It was difficult not to wonder if it might have links with Parker's review, though I told myself that it was highly unlikely that anyone in town was a subscriber.

Aside from a certain guest, that is. "I wonder if Sofia has left yet?"

"I haven't seen her since yesterday, so I'm guessing not," Jia said. "I bet she's seen this newest update, though."

"I didn't expect it to escalate like this." I scanned the near-empty restaurant, guilt ballooning in my chest. "Maybe we should have put out a public statement after Jonas's death after all."

"To say what?" Jia asked. "That would have only drawn more attention."

"I agree," Mart put in from behind us. "Where is everyone? It's deader than me in here."

"Ha ha," I said sourly. "I haven't the faintest idea, but it's not that unusual for it to be quiet on a Monday morning."

"You didn't find Jonas's ghost either?" asked my brother.

"No, I didn't." Irritation prickled beneath my skin. "Guess he moved on."

As for his widow…

"Where are you going?" Jia asked as I ducked out from behind the bar. "To talk to Allie? I already told her about the update on Parker's blog."

"I want to ask if she's heard from Esther today." It wouldn't be a bad idea to check if she knew when Sofia was leaving too.

"Hey," Allie said from behind the front desk when I walked into the lobby. "Another quiet day?"

"For now," I said. "Have you seen Sofia yet?"

"She's checking out later today," she replied. "No, she isn't on the next tour. I checked."

"One is enough for her to steal our ideas," I muttered. "I guess you can't trademark a tour, but still. Have you heard from Esther?"

"No," she replied. "I was worried too. I called the hospital, and they said they transferred her husband's body home as she'd requested. With luck, she won't be back anytime soon."

"She hasn't been in touch with the police, then?" Drew would know, so I pulled out my phone to message him. "I know Drew has more sense than to let slip to Esther what I told him yesterday, but Jonas's ghost was a no-show, so any chance of getting his account of his own death has crashed and burned."

Allie studied me. "You tried to summon his ghost?"

"I tried both kinds of summonings but with no luck. He must have moved on."

"You really think it was a ghost that caused his death?" Her expression shadowed. "If anyone finds out, they'll assume it was one of *our* ghosts regardless of the circumstances. We can't let any word of this reach Esther, Maura."

"I haven't told a soul except for you and Drew. Oh, and Jia, but you know she wouldn't tell anyone."

Carey might have worked it out too. She was intelligent, and I couldn't pull the wool over her eyes about my suspicions for much longer.

"All right." Concern laced her voice. "I know you want answers, but please be careful. If Esther finds out anything that she can use against us…"

"I know," I said. "I'll be careful, but with that Parker posting lies about us, I can't promise she won't stumble upon the truth anyway."

Though I didn't even know what the truth *was*, frankly. There was no chance a regular ghost could have committed murder, and my own experience told me they were terrible at following orders too. As Sofia had turned out to be a dead end, I was out of ideas on the perpetrator's identity too.

"Jia told me he blocked you from emailing him, so I'd not try to find another way to get in contact. It'll only antagonise him further."

I had an inkling it was a little too late to prevent that particular boulder from rolling downhill, but I refrained from saying so aloud. "I won't, don't worry."

I ducked back into the restaurant and found Jia leaning on the bar and staring at her phone screen.

"Oh boy, did he reply?" I asked.

"No... he deleted my comment," she said. "And blocked me from posting again."

"Seriously?" I grabbed my own phone and began to type out a comment, though it was likely to have the same result. What was his problem? Did he simply not want to have a public argument, or was he trying to avoid talking to us at all? I'd guess the latter, given that he'd prevented us from emailing him, too, but I didn't think our request to remove the pictures of Jonas's body had been unreasonable. "Does he have nothing better to do with his time?"

"Apparently not," Jia said. "I'd like to think some people saw my comment before it disappeared, but that might be too much to ask of the universe."

"They might have, if his site gets as much traffic as he claims."

It also struck me that we might have been doing more useful things with our day than having a passive-aggressive online standoff, so I messaged Drew and asked if he'd heard from Esther. No response came, but several minutes later, the restaurant door opened, and several customers came in.

"Good," I murmured. "We're not pariahs after all."

"Yet," Mart said helpfully. "Parker isn't going to pay either of you any attention, but if you change your mind, I'd be happy to go and haunt him in person. That'll teach him."

At this point I was tempted to tell him to go ahead, but there was another hitch. "I don't know where he lives."

We had no chance of resolving this one face-to-face unless he came back to the inn, which would bring a whole host of other problems. I did my best to put the issue to the back of my mind and focused on serving our customers instead, though the restaurant remained quieter than typical for a weekday. I couldn't help wondering how Carey was getting on at school too. We hadn't discussed tomorrow's tour all weekend, and I had the suspicion that her classmates' reaction might prove the tipping point as to whether she'd decide to go ahead with it.

I didn't get a reply from Drew until later that morning. He sent an ominous response telling me that he'd had a call from Esther and that he'd be in touch later to give me the details.

"What's that mean?" I frowned at my phone. "Esther called the police again... why?"

"She didn't, did she?" Jia, for unfathomable reasons, had been scrolling through Parker's blog during gaps between serving customers. "What for?"

"Nothing good, I assume." I'd assumed her ongoing scheme to sink our business and the pitfalls I'd experienced when trying to track Jonas's ghost were unconnected, but what if I was mistaken? Esther couldn't see ghosts herself, but her militant persistence in the face of any available evidence made me wonder if there was more to her accusations than met the eye. "Why would Esther assume a ghost killed her husband in the first place?"

"Well, she *was* on a ghost tour," said Jia. "You think she was able to see them all along?"

"No... I don't know." Frustrated, I paced behind the bar. "It seems weird for her to be so adamant that a ghost killed him and yet so utterly unconcerned with finding out which ghost it was. I realise she's no Reaper, but she must be aware that ghosts generally have a will of their own, right?"

"Well, yes," she said. "Wait—do you think she knew her husband was being tailed by a murderous ghost? Or did she set the ghost on him herself and is trying to cover her tracks by accusing our ghosts instead?"

"I don't know, I'm just throwing out ideas," I said. "I think it's safe to say that it wasn't a regular ghost, and if it came here with the purpose of murdering someone, why would it choose him?"

"You're asking the wrong person." With a sudden curse, Jia dropped her phone, causing it to clatter onto the counter. "He's got to be kidding."

"What?" I could guess who she meant by 'he,' and sure enough, when I opened up Parker's blog, I nearly dropped *my* phone. A new headline topped the page.

Coming soon: an exclusive interview with Esther Wrigley, widow of the victim who met a tragic end at the grand opening of the Riverside Inn's ghost tours.

"He's interviewing her?" I said incredulously. "What is she thinking?"

Jia's head slumped over her phone. "Read the rest of the post. It's bad."

I read on, and dread gripped me with every word. *Our interview will cover a number of important questions concerning the incident at the Riverside Inn. For instance, we have reason to believe that there is currently a rogue Reaper working at the inn. Yes, you read that right... a Reaper.*

"He... he knows I'm a Reaper."

He might not know *I* specifically was the Reaper, but who'd tipped him off that there was one working here at all? More to the point, did he have any idea of the level of risk he'd invoked by publicly sharing that information? The Reaper Council made MI5 look like an open book.

"How?" asked Jia. "I guess any local might have told him, but if Esther knows, too, then she'll be even more inclined to think her husband's death wasn't an accident."

"He might be planning to tell her at the interview," I said slowly. "We could gate-crash and explain to her that he's setting her up."

"Would she listen, though?"

"Not to me." What the hell was he playing at? Was he actively trying to get me into trouble with the Reaper Council? Not only was my status as a Reaper not supposed to be known outside of Hawkwood Hollow, but there was a difference between casually telling an acquaintance and announcing it to three thousand followers across the globe. If the Reaper Council leapt to the conclusion that I *was* a rogue, then they'd shut down our tours and maybe even the inn too.

Mart cleared his throat. "I told you I'll go and haunt him for you. Just give me the word, and *I'll* gate-crash the interview."

"He can't see or hear you, though," I reminded him. "Neither can Esther. No, we have to go and find them ourselves."

I assumed they planned to meet in public, but where? I could technically use my Reaper powers to search for Parker, but only if he was within a certain range. Besides, walking out of the shadows and landing in the middle of their interview would not exactly help my case.

Something had to be done, though. Jonas's ghost was gone, and whether his death had been an accident or not, the blame would land squarely on us if my Reaper status spread any further.

We had to act fast.

8

To start off with, I needed to find out what Drew had heard from Esther earlier, so I sent a message saying I needed to talk to him. Urgently.

Drew called back within five minutes. "Hey, Maura. Sorry if my message earlier worried you."

"Did Esther mention she's going to do an interview with Parker Maven, by any chance? You know, that blogger?"

"She told me she planned to talk to the press," he said. "That might be what she meant, but there's nothing I can do to stop her."

"What else did she say?"

"You can probably imagine, if she's said the same to Allie," he said. "She wants justice for her husband, and she's utterly convinced you set a murderous ghost on her."

"Me personally?" I gripped the phone. "Because Parker's blog mentioned that there's a rogue Reaper working at the inn. Didn't say my name, but you know why I can't let that spread any further."

He swore. "That I didn't know. Esther didn't mention you by name, Maura, but if she knows…"

"Then she'll have twice the reason to shut us down *and* get me into serious trouble with the Reaper Council," I finished, my heart racing with adrenaline. "Parker has blocked me and Jia from commenting on his blog and contacting him via email, so we have no other way to get hold of him. I don't want to force an in-person confrontation, but if anyone connected to the Reapers sees that post of his, then they might show up at the inn. Then? Either I get arrested, we get shut down, or both."

"I won't let them do that," Drew said firmly. "I tried to talk sense into Esther, but she was adamant, and if this Parker has offered her the publicity she desires, then I'm not surprised she took him up on the offer."

"Yes, but this isn't going to bring her any closer to the answers she's looking for," I said. "Though I had another thought earlier... what if she's making these accusations because she's trying to divert the blame? If the spirit that killed Jonas hitched a ride to Hawkwood Hollow with him and his wife, then I can see why she'd want to find someone else to accuse instead."

"I don't know about that, Maura," he said. "The police aren't investigating his death as a murder, and if we were, it would lend Esther's claims more legitimacy. I know you don't want to take that risk."

"Yeah, but I figured I should let you know my theories," I said. "You know, in case I'm hauled off by the Reaper Council before I can find out the truth."

"Maura, please don't say that," he said. "If there's anything in my power that I can do to stop them from coming here, then please let me know."

Oops. I hadn't meant to panic him, though my flippant tone disguised genuine fear. "Drew, it'll be okay. I should tell Allie what's going on and let you get back to work, but if you can find out which town Parker lives in, it might help me figure out where he's planning to do this interview."

"So you can gate-crash?"

He knew me too well. "Not necessarily. If it's a magical community, then I can find out if there are any Reapers I need to worry about if I have the name."

"I'll do my best to find out," he said. "Talk soon?"

"Sure." I ended the call and then jogged into the reception area.

Allie's gaze snapped up from her computer. "It's bad news, isn't it?"

"Esther is going to do an exclusive interview with Parker," I told her. "She also called the police earlier and told them she was going to talk to the press."

She lowered her gaze. "I was afraid she'd do something like this. Monetary compensation was never going to be enough for her."

"She… she's going to find out I'm a Reaper, if she doesn't already know." For some reason it was harder to tell her than it was anyone else, perhaps because Allie was the person likely to end up in the deep end if the Reaper Council perceived her as having helped me evade the law. "Parker said that they're going to discuss the rumour that there's a rogue Reaper working at the inn, so if she doesn't already now, then she will soon."

The colour drained from her face, and my insides clenched. "What… what can we do?"

"I'm waiting for Drew to find out their meeting place," I explained. "If I can find one of them first, then I can explain that the Reaper Council will hang them out to dry for exposing their secrets. Even Parker won't be able to get away from that one."

That wouldn't stop him from sharing the rest of their interview, of course, but Parker had no idea what kind of bear he was poking by plastering the word "Reaper" all over his blog. Really, I was doing him a favour by putting a stop to him.

"Is it likely that they'll find out?" she asked. "The Reaper Council? I know you've mentioned them before, but I don't think you've ever fully explained their rules…"

"The main rule is secrecy above all else," I said. "It's not usual for anyone to leave their ranks, let alone set up a ghost-tour business, so we could land in trouble if they jump to conclusions about what's going on here."

"Which of us?"

"All of us, especially me." I shuddered. "They're barely human. In fact, by all definitions, they aren't. There's a reason they talk of the Grim Reaper and not the Happy Reaper. But that's the worst-case scenario, and I doubt they make a habit of lurking on the internet, reading ghost-tour blogs. I intend to scare the hell out of Parker before he lets the situation escalate any further."

I'd probably scared the hell out of her, too, so I left it at that. Maybe I was overreacting—the notoriously techno-phobic Reaper Council didn't even own mobile phones, let alone have access to the internet—but they weren't entirely cut off from the outside world.

If anything, I needed to talk to the town's *actual* Reaper, but not before I'd tried to stop Parker's interview before it got off the ground.

Back in the restaurant, I found Jia scrolling through Parker's blog. I left her to it and got on with serving customers until she exclaimed, "Aha!"

"Huh?"

"I figured out where Parker lives," she said triumphantly. "Littlewood. It's the next town over from this one, just to the northeast."

"Are you sure?"

"Positive," she replied. "Can't say I know his address, but it's a small town, and if Parker and Esther are meeting up in public, then you might be able to find them. Can you use your Reaper skills to get there quickly?"

"Possibly, but there's a chance I might accidentally land on top of them."

Mart cackled with laughter. "She's done it before. There are a few occasions I could mention when the person in question was taking a shower."

"Oi," I warned him. "This is serious."

"You need to chill out."

"You're the one whose literal existence will be at stake if another Reaper sees that blog post," I pointed out. "If we get cornered by the council, the first thing they'll do is banish you to the permanent afterworld."

They might do the same to the other ghosts at the inn too. To be honest, Jonathan and the others had had a good reason to flee, but that didn't mean I intended to give up the fight. Even if it involved risking further humiliation by pursuing Parker and Esther.

I turned to Jia. "Fancy a ride on the Reaper Express? Or would you rather stay and keep an eye out for a certain ex-coven member?"

She glanced over at the door to the lobby. "I think one of us should stay here. Just in case someone's counting on you leaving."

"Never even thought of that." There were too many possibilities, and the tornado of paranoia in my mind was held in check only by my determination to stop Parker's interview in its tracks. "Okay, you hold the fort. Good luck."

I didn't blame Jia for wanting to stay behind, not least because travel with a Reaper was not exactly what one would call a comfortable experience. I didn't normally bring other people along for the ride at all—with one obvious exception.

I gave Mart a look, and he sighed. "Fine. You owe me for this."

"You don't want the Reaper Council here any more than I do, do you? Besides, I need help judging the distance."

Littlewood wasn't far from Hawkwood Hollow, but I didn't actually know how far my Reaper skills stretched, and I didn't want to find the limit the hard way and land feetfirst in a lake.

As Mart drifted to my side, I pictured the country lane leading out of Hawkwood Hollow, but my phone buzzed in my pocket, unbalancing me. I caught the desk with my hand to avoid tripping and saw Drew was calling me.

"Ah—hey, Drew," I answered. "Er, there's no need to find the address. We already know where Parker and Esther are."

"Maura... don't go to Littlewood." I had to strain my ears to hear him, since he spoke quietly and the murmur of several other voices came from the background.

"Why?" I gripped the phone. "Drew, why?"

"Because," he replied, "Parker was found dead less than ten minutes ago, according to his housemate. I called his mobile phone and found out he died of apparent heart failure."

My own heart gave a lurch. "Wait—before he went to meet Esther?"

"Yes. I don't know if Esther is aware yet, but it strikes me as a bad idea for any of us to contact her at the moment."

"No kidding."

It sounded as if Parker had died in the same manner as Jonas had, so showing up in Littlewood would paint a glaring target on my own head. As long as Esther didn't find out that we'd planned to intercept her, she couldn't make the connection, but that didn't mean she wouldn't try.

When I ended the call, Jia glanced at me. "Bad news?"

"You might say that. Parker is dead. I'm pretty sure whatever killed Jonas got him too."

She swore. "Seriously? The same ghost?"

"I'd hazard a guess at a yes." Unless there were multiple ghosts running around with the capacity to murder people, anyway. "He never even made it to the interview."

Jia gave a low whistle. "Well, that puts a dent in our plans. Or Esther's. Does she know?"

"Drew doesn't think so, and I don't want to enlighten her." It was bad enough that we'd planned to go to Littlewood at all, though at least our small number of customers hadn't overheard our plans. "If the authorities find out about our disagreement, it might cause issues."

Jia cursed under her breath. "Wait, what'll happen to his blog? I assume it'll stay up indefinitely?"

"Exactly." His review of the inn would stay up publicly until someone said otherwise, which might be never. He might not have left instructions for his blog after his death, since he hadn't expected to die. As a professional ghost hunter, one would think the possibility would have crossed his mind, but his arrogant attitude when we'd met had suggested that he would never have believed he'd meet his end at the hands of a spirit.

Jia pursed her lips. "I wonder if we can get into his website and remove that post? Or at least amend it to remove the reference to the Reapers?"

"Maybe." I swivelled towards my brother. "You're good at figuring out passwords. Mine, anyway. Can you do the same for him?"

"I'm not working for free," he said. "Forget it."

"The longer that review stays up on the web, the more likely it is that someone will see it and decide to pick up where Parker left off," I told him. "I just want to remove the reference to my Reaper status. If you won't do it for free, then we can discuss compensation after it's down."

"Agreed," said Jia. "Come on, Mart, you can't deny it'll be fun for you to screw around with his blog."

"Fine." He gave a long-suffering sigh. "Don't say I never do you any favours. Give me your phone."

I placed the phone down on the counter in front of him. "Please don't mess with anything else on there."

"You mean I can't change your background picture to a photo of you as an infant?"

"Not the time, Mart." Though I'd happily tolerate any of his antics as long as that blog post was erased, or at the very least stripped of all references to the Reapers.

As for Parker himself, it'd be a while before *his* ghost showed up, and for all I knew, he'd disappear in the interim just like Jonas had. Even if not, I couldn't count on him being any more reasonable as a ghost than he'd been as a living person.

While Mart got to work trying out passwords, I went into the lobby to tell Allie the bad news.

"I thought you were leaving," she said. "Did Drew call?"

"Yeah, and our blogger met with an unfortunate end."

Her eyes rounded. "Parker's dead?"

"Yep," I said. "Apparently, he dropped dead of a heart attack."

"Like Jonas. The same cause."

"Yeah, but since he was nowhere near the inn, I don't see how anyone can possibly blame us for this one." Including Esther, but that wasn't to say she wouldn't try. "Mart is trying to get into Parker's blog account so he can remove all references to the Reapers."

"I wouldn't do any more than that," she said seriously. "If anyone makes the connection between your recent argument... it's lucky he wasn't at the inn when he died."

"Precisely my thinking." I wouldn't shed a tear for him, though, and if not for my secrets being at risk of exposure and the inn's reputation being on the line, I would be content to forget all about him. "Do you want to tell Carey, or should I?"

"You can tell her, but—be gentle with her."

She'd already known about the review, of course, but I'd see how her day at school had gone before I dropped any more bombshells on her. Jia agreed, so we resolved to act as if everything were normal until Mart managed to hack his way into Parker's blog and delete the evidence.

When Carey came into the restaurant at the end of the school day, she appeared mildly subdued but not devastated, from which I deduced that she'd escaped lightly.

"How was your day?" Jia asked her.

"Not too bad," Carey said. "What about yours?"

"Eventful." I opted to be honest but brief. "Your class-mates—they didn't give you any trouble?"

"Believe it or not, they were supportive," she said. "I think someone must have spoken to Cris and her friends, because she didn't say anything to me at all."

I glanced over at Allie, who'd just entered, and the brief flicker of guilt in her expression hinted that she'd been the culprit. I was glad Carey's classmates had left her alone regardless, but how to break the news? Her gaze drifted towards the counter, where my phone flickered seemingly of its own accord as Mart tried to get into Parker's blog.

"What did you mean by 'eventful'?" asked Carey. "Seri-ously, you can tell me if there's bad news. I'd rather know sooner than later."

"Parker…" I paused. "You know he posted lies about us on his blog? Well… he won't be doing that any longer."

"Why?" Then she gasped. "He's dead?"

"Don't worry, it has nothing to do with us," I reassured her. "He wasn't anywhere near Hawkwood Hollow when he died. Mart's trying to get into his website to take down that review of his, because otherwise it'll stay up there indefinitely, but we don't have anything to worry about."

She paled. "What do you mean? If he's dead, then... then was he killed by the same ghost that got Jonas?"

"We don't even know he was killed by a ghost," said Jia.

Carey lowered her gaze, her hands trembling. "It *is* possible, isn't it?"

"Ghosts can't kill people," I said. "Regular ghosts can't, anyway. Besides, the authorities can't possibly blame us for the death of someone who wasn't anywhere near our property at the time."

"They can," she insisted. "How'd you find out he died?"

Oh boy. So much for breaking the news to her gently, but she might as well know exactly what pernicious secrets Mart was attempting to erase.

When I'd finished explaining the day's developments, she sank into a seat at the nearest table. "The Reapers might come here and shut us down? Really?"

"Nope." Behind the counter, Mart did a triumphant dance. "Guess who finally got into his account?"

"Really?" I ran over to check my phone, and sure enough, he did indeed seem to have logged into Parker's website. "It wasn't hard to guess his password?"

"No, it seems obvious now," he said. "Turns out he used his own name. Even I don't think *that* highly of myself."

"Nice going," Jia said. "Want to take down that review? Carey?"

"I can take it down or rewrite it to sing our praises," Mart said. "What do you think?"

Jia gave Carey a questioning look, and she said, "Get rid of it, if you can. Delete the whole page."

"Agreed." The sooner we buried this whole matter, the better.

"Your wish is my command." Mart tapped my phone's

screen with a flourish, and the topmost post on the blog vanished—photos, comments, and all.

"That's enough of that," said Jia. "Now we can put this all behind us."

Yes. That ought to be the end of it... except for two people being dead, but since I hadn't liked either of them, it wasn't as if I ought to be in a hurry to find their killer. I'd caused Drew enough stress today already.

"What if the police find out he stayed at the inn and attended the ghost tour?" Carey's smile faded. "What if they come asking questions?"

"Drew said it sounds like he died of a heart attack," I said. "If that's the official story, then the police in Littlewood won't have any reason to come here. They certainly won't make the connection with Jonas."

"Also, Esther was trying to blame our ghosts for her husband's death," added Jia. "Not only are our ghosts all accounted for, but the odds of any of them being about to scoot over to Littlewood are pretty much non-existent."

"Exactly," I said. "This might be a good thing for us, eventually."

"Not with a killer on the loose," Carey murmured. "A killer nobody can see."

Except a Reaper, a voice whispered in the back of my head, which wasn't entirely inaccurate. I did have the skills needed to find and banish this mysterious murderous ghost, except nobody was paying me, and if I tried to go solo, I was more likely to take the blame myself.

No, I was better off staying out of this one.

Thanks to the rest of the day's events, I'd utterly forgotten we had a tour tomorrow to prepare for until Allie came in with her clipboard towards the end of our shift.

"How many people do we have on tomorrow's tour?" I asked her.

"Not as many as the first night, but more than enough for a full tour," she replied. "I didn't expect us to get as many bookings tomorrow either way, since we had almost all our potential local audience attend on Friday."

"Yeah, and it's the middle of the week too," Jia said. "It's bound to vary from tour to tour, but we still have more than enough people booked in."

Carey nodded, though traces of worry remained in her expression. "Aren't we going to do anything to stop a repeat of the first night? If there are any more accidents, even minor ones, people might get the same idea as Esther did."

"We'll give out health and safety forms," Jia said promptly. "Like I said, Esther is bound to give up her crusade in the end, but at least we've covered our backs this time."

"Exactly," I said. "And I'll keep both eyes out for any signs of trouble. That's all I can do."

As for the other ghosts, I'd decided not to tell them of Parker's unfortunate demise. It might upset them to find out that their fears hadn't been unfounded, but Parker hadn't been anywhere near the inn at the time and neither had his killer. We didn't need anyone else pulling a disappearing act before tomorrow's tour.

"Same here," said Jia. "Look, Carey, forget Esther. Forget Parker too. We're going to prove that we can bounce back from any misfortune, stronger than ever. Deal?"

"Yes, we can," I added, despite my lingering suspicions that the timing of Parker's death might end up coming back to bite me if someone got wind of our enmity. "Someone" meaning Esther.

At least the word "Reaper" was no longer floating around the internet in connection to the inn, and there was nothing more to do. Like Mart had said, it was time to put this behind us.

9

T he universe disagreed. A sleepless Allie greeted me at the desk when I came downstairs the next morning. "Esther called again."

"You've got to be joking," I said. "What did she say?"

"She claimed that once she's done sorting out her husband's funeral and affairs, she'll return her attention to getting justice for him." Her mouth was set in a grim line. "I don't think she's going to let this one drop."

"Has she heard about Parker's death, do you know?"

"She didn't mention him, but she did say she had an interview arranged with the press."

I swore. "She must have come up with a backup plan. Or booked several interviews back-to-back."

Evidently, she hadn't made the connection between Parker's death and her husband's demise, but that didn't matter if she remained fixated on the inn regardless of any available evidence.

"That's what I thought," she said. "I didn't want to be the one to bring up the subject of Parker's blog, given that you intended to go to interrupt the interview yourself."

I grimaced. "I know. What were we supposed to do, though, let him get away with provoking the Reaper Council?"

Allie studied my face. "It wasn't *them* who silenced him, was it?"

"Definitely not." I suppressed a reflexive shudder. "They don't kill the living unless they have a *very* good reason. That's one of our laws too. Most likely they'd have pressured him to take down the post, but they'd have come to the inn first. We had a lucky escape."

There was no point in downplaying the issue: the crime of harbouring a rogue Reaper was a margin higher than posting a blog post about it, though both would draw the Council's ire. I *hoped* Esther hadn't read the post before it disappeared. The last thing we needed was her spreading the same rumour to every news outlet and blog willing to interview her.

Allie sucked in a breath. "You think the victims both died of the same cause, don't you? They were murdered."

"Not by the typical kind of murderer, but yes, I do." Coincidences were a rare thing in my experience, especially when it came to the dead. "Most spirits aren't even strong enough to poke a person in the arm, let alone induce a heart attack, so I can't think how they did it."

"Esther doesn't know anything about ghosts either," she said. "I wish there was a way to resolve this without giving her another reason to target us."

"Same here." Despite my resolve to keep my attention on tonight's upcoming ghost tour, the subject had remained in the back of my mind since yesterday, including the mystery of how our disembodied killer had got from Hawkwood Hollow all the way to Littlewood. And if Esther herself had been in Littlewood at the time, then she was the one connecting factor between the two victims. "If she was willing to have a civilised conversation, we might have been able to help her. Instead, we have two people dead, and she's intent on pursuing the wrong target."

Allie cleared her throat. "Speaking of targets, is it possible that the killer was waiting to ambush her when they killed Parker. Or... or you?"

"Me?" I echoed. "I doubt the ghost knew I was coming to interrupt their interview."

The notion of Esther being the intended target was an interesting one, though, and Allie had most likely been up half the night going through possible scenarios, the same as I had.

"No... I suppose not," she said. "I sometimes wish I had more than a rudimentary knowledge of ghosts, given that we're running tours now, but if even *you* don't know what it is, Maura..."

"I freely admit I've forgotten most of my Reaper lessons," I said in an attempt to reassure her. "Besides, the ghostly killer isn't anywhere near Hawkwood Hollow, and I doubt any of us was the intended target."

I hadn't even considered the possibility that Jonas hadn't been the spirit's original target at all, thanks to Esther's insistence on keeping all the attention on herself and her husband. Maybe Esther herself had been the target after all.

"Where did the spirit come from?" asked Allie. "The afterworld, I assume, but it can't have decided to kill people of its own accord."

"Yeah, odds are high that someone summoned it," I said. "Ghosts can have a will of their own, but they can't get here without help."

Sofia's face came to mind, but we hadn't found any evidence in her room upstairs that she'd been dabbling in illegal magic. The coven's involvement couldn't be ruled out, though.

"The police can arrest the summoner if they catch them, but what about the ghost?" she asked. "Would that be the Reaper Council's responsibility?"

"They only get involved if a Reaper did the actual summoning," I said. "Otherwise... well, it depends if there's anyone in the area who knows how to deal with monsters from the afterworld. It's not exactly a common skill."

Outside of the Reapers, there were two groups of specialists in the magical world who dealt with magical threats: the paranormal hunters and the Wardens. The former were usually regular humans with a couple of advantages that enabled them to see the magical world, while the latter comprised a variety of paranormals who inexplicably *enjoyed* dealing with magical monsters on a regular basis. Very few hunters could see ghosts, and while the Wardens were a more likely bet, there was no guarantee the local branch contained anyone with the skills to deal with a rogue spirit from the afterworld. Despite their many pitfalls, that ability mostly resided with the Reapers. Including me—and old Harold.

Well, I had to talk to him eventually.

Since I still had a while before my shift started, I resigned myself to the joyous task of telling our resident grumpy Reaper that I'd almost been arrested by the Council. Without further ado, I left the inn and walked over the bridge, while Mart drifted along behind me, singing to himself.

"Why're you in such a good mood?" I asked him.

"I get to entertain the public again tonight," he said. "You *are* still going ahead with the tour, aren't you? Despite Esther's endless supply of hot air?"

"As far as I know, yes." Allie hadn't said otherwise, but I'd probably freaked her out when I'd given her honest answers to her questions concerning our disembodied killer. I had to admit getting Harold to acknowledge the issue was a long shot, but my patchy knowledge of the afterworld's many monsters was a major stumbling block to figuring out what we were dealing with. Now the hospital had sent Jonas's body home, I'd lost the chance to find out if there'd been any physical signs pointing to his killer's identity, but that had been a long shot anyway.

No, the cause was in the afterworld, and like it or not, Harold was the person to talk to when it came to matters involving incorporeal killers.

The town's only cemetery covered a sloping grassy hill, at the foot of which sat the Reaper's cottage. Numbered 42 despite its lack of neighbours, it had grimy windows that masked its interior, and the painted door was faded with age.

I rapped my knuckles on the wooden surface and received the customary answer: "Go away."

"Lovely to see you too," I said to the Reaper. "I imagine you heard the latest news?"

"If you mean the unfortunate demise of your ghost-tour venture, then I could have warned you myself that it was doomed to failure. Involving spirits in one's business plans is bound to end in disaster."

"You're such a ray of sunshine, you know that?" I rolled my eyes at the closed door. "For your information, our business is doing just fine, but there seems to be a disembodied killer on the loose in the area, so I thought you ought to know."

"Didn't you vet the ghosts before you hired them?"

"Hey, it wasn't one of *our* ghosts," I said. "Have you ever heard of a spirit that can cause a person to drop dead without any obvious cause?"

"Yes, a parasitic spirit or demon," he growled. "What have you brought upon us this time?"

Demon. That was a term I hadn't heard for a while. "I didn't bring anything here. It's not even *in* town."

"Then it's not your problem, is it?"

"Esther's trying to prosecute the inn for our supposed responsibility in her husband's death," I said. "He was killed by that—demon, or whatever it was—and it claimed a second victim in Littlewood yesterday. The second victim was trying to get us into trouble with the Reaper Council before he met his untimely death. *That* is my problem."

"It's also a risk you took when you opened that business."

"You sent that Shelton off to placate the council yourself," I pointed out. "I thought you didn't mind me staying."

"I very much mind your habit of bringing dangerous spirits into the region."

"What part of *it wasn't one of our ghosts* do you not understand?" My hands curled into fists. "I've done my level best to keep a low profile, but as long as that creature is on the loose, there's a chance it might come back to Hawkwood Hollow. All I wanted to know was what we're dealing with."

"I told you what you're dealing with," he said. "It's not my problem if you paid no attention in your Reaper lessons."

The term "demon" covered a wide range of spirits, though, and it still left the thorny issue of who'd summoned the damn thing in the first place.

"You can't have a demon without a summoner," I said. "Also, I'm pretty sure they didn't summon it in Hawkwood Hollow."

"Then like I said, it's none of your—"

"It's my business if people die on our ghost tours and try to pin the blame on the inn," I interjected. "Hypothetically, if I tried to hunt down this creature myself, are there any signs I should look out for? It left no traces behind, and only the other ghosts noticed its presence, so tracking it is going to be a challenge."

He scoffed. "Then you weren't looking hard enough. The

afterworld always tells the truth. I would have thought you'd know that."

"I wasn't looking because I didn't *know* it was there." I might as well have tried to reason with Esther for all the good it did, but in between his barbed comments, he'd given me enough information to work with.

Old Harold and I had a shaky history, but despite his grumpiness, he'd ensured I had a future in Hawkwood Hollow, even if he wanted to do his level best to avoid admitting it. For that reason alone, I was fairly sure he'd step in to help me if the Reaper Council did show up... but only at the last possible moment.

"I told you what you want to know," he said. "Will you go away now?"

"One more question," I said. "Why didn't the demon come after me? Wasn't I the most obvious target?" If the demon was of the parasitic variety, then it fed on a person's life energy, and one would have thought it wouldn't have been able to resist such an obvious target.

"Because Reapers are immune, of course."

Oh. "Right."

It had slipped my mind, but Reapers were immune to all kinds of ghost-related nastiness. We wouldn't last very long in the afterworld if the ghosts could kill us.

"Obviously," he said. "And if you want to know why the demon picked out its victims, you need to ask people who knew them."

"He kind of has a point this time," Mart put in, as I turned away from the cottage. "I wonder if that Esther knew her husband had a demonic hitchhiker?"

"We don't know that's how it got to town." Though I'd already wondered if the monster's choice of target hadn't been random. Why would it then go after Parker, though? He and Esther hadn't known each other before he'd offered her an interview, or so I'd thought. "Can you imagine what Esther would say if I asked her?"

I debated the merits of risking her wrath while Mart and I walked back to the inn from the cemetery. Esther was determined to remain a thorn in our side, but if we wanted to find out why her husband had been targeted, then we might have to take the risk of talking to her again. I needed to check in with Drew at some point too.

I returned to the inn and saw that Jia had already shown up for her shift.

"I wondered where you'd gone," she said when I joined her at the bar. "I heard Esther was up to her usual nonsense earlier."

"Yeah, she called Allie and yelled at her," I said. "I just went to visit our delightful local Reaper."

Her brows rose. "Was it worth it?"

"Kind of," I said. "I mean, he gave me an idea of what kind of ghostly serial killer we're dealing with, but he also refused outright to get involved and discouraged me from doing the same."

"Did you really expect him to leap on the chance to help us out?"

Mart answered for me. "Yes. She doesn't like to admit it, but she's an optimist at heart."

"Oi," I said. "I like to call myself more of a realist. Besides, it's hard to know what to expect from him. I thought the threat of the Reaper Council showing up on the doorstep might be an incentive, but I guess not."

"It sounds like he did give you some information, though," said Jia. "What kind of monster is it?"

"A demon. Or demonic spirit, if you want the technical term, though the word covers a bunch of different creatures with similar abilities."

Demonic spirits were classified by their strength. The

strongest could take control of a person's body and manipu-late it against their will, while the weakest couldn't do much more than drain a person's will to live... which was still unappealing.

"Whoa," she said. "They can kill people without even touching them?"

"Except Reapers," I said. "I think the demon must only be able to target one person at any given time, given how spaced out its victims were. He mentioned it was likely a parasite of some kind. The sort that feeds on someone's life force."

"Whoa," Jia said. "That's why the ghosts disappeared."

A chill raced down my spine. "You think so?"

"I mean, I'm not an expert on demons," she said. "But you've mentioned other beasts from the afterworld that have some similar abilities, haven't you?"

True. I'd had several run-ins with hellbeasts, which fed on ghosts' life forces... though not while their spirits were still attached to a living body. If the demon had sucked out Jonas's life force, it would explain why I hadn't been able to find his ghost.

"The real stumbling block is how to *find* it," I said. "A generic summoning spell might work, but it's a hell of a risk."

"Isn't there another regional Reaper who can deal with this, instead of you?"

"I wouldn't count on it," I replied. "The Reaper Council doesn't get involved unless the demon starts massacring normals or something else that might expose them to the public at large. A couple of deaths isn't enough to get their attention."

"Lovely." A furrow appeared in her brow. "You *aren't* going to hunt it down yourself, are you?"

"Not before I know who summoned it." Demons varied in terms of intelligence, but the lesser ones tended to obey their summoner's commands. "Honestly, I thought Esther might have a few more clues to drop. She's the one person who connects the two victims, aside from me."

"You still think she had her husband murdered?" she asked. "Then why would she go to all this trouble to discredit us?"

"I don't know," I said. "She was in Littlewood before Parker died, too, and I have a hard time believing that's a coincidence."

"Now you mention it, I have an idea of why Parker was targeted," she said. "I read more of his blog…"

"And you didn't want to gouge your eyes out?"

"It felt like swimming in sewage, to be honest, but I was part of the coven, so that's nothing new."

"Ha," I said. "What did you find out?"

"Turns out he has a habit of riling up any ghosts he stumbles across," she said. "He has no more respect for the dead than the living. If you ask me, he ticked off someone he shouldn't have and got himself into trouble."

"Too bad we can't ask him." If a demon had devoured his spirit, then there'd be nothing left of his ghost to summon. "Esther might be able to shed some light on the situation, though, and we have her number."

"Yeah, because she's trying to sink our business," she said. "For the record, I think you're right, but isn't making contact with her bound to end in disaster?"

"Not if we approach it the right way."

I was fast running out of possible ways to pin down the summoner, and unlike Parker, Esther was still very much alive. If she was the next intended victim, she might be grateful for my warning… or not. *Hmm. Maybe Mart is right. Part of me is an optimist at heart after all.*

10

I opted to call Drew before I spoke to Esther. I'd already intended to talk to him before that evening's tour to discuss the possibility of him helping us with extra security in case Esther came back or someone else decided to make trouble, but when he didn't answer his phone, I assumed he must be busy at work. I fired off a message with a brief explanation of my discussion with the Reaper and then went to put my suggestion to Allie instead.

Needless to say, she wasn't a fan of the idea.

"I don't think that's a good idea, Maura," she said. "If you call Esther yourself, then you're giving her another opening to come after the inn."

"I know, but what if she knows something important?" I asked. "That demon has killed two people, and she's the sole connecting factor."

Except for me, of course, and the fact that I was immune to the demon's attack didn't mean I hadn't been the target. That, or someone wanted me to take the fall. We'd slowed down the inevitable by removing Parker's blog post alluding to my Reaper status, but if Esther remained determined to talk to the press, someone else might pick up where he left off.

Allie's brow wrinkled. "You think she's the person who summoned it? Or was she the original target?"

"Either. Or neither." I shook my head. "That's the trouble. We don't know nearly enough, but it's too late to question Parker and find out what *he* knew. Jia said he had a habit of riling up ghosts."

"Or summoning them?" she queried. "Ah—what's the difference between a demon and a regular ghost?"

"It's more of a terminology thing." That and it was more reassuring to lump all the spirits whose abilities fell under the "mind-numbingly terrifying" umbrella into the same category, as distinct from the relatively harmless spirits that were a more everyday sight. "Demons...unlike ghosts, they don't have any resemblance to the people they used to be when they were alive, though they have some abilities in common with regular ghosts."

"And they can... they can kill living people?"

"Some can," I said delicately, not wanting to freak her out any more than I already had. "But there are conditions. The one we're dealing with... Harold thinks it's a parasite. It feeds on the life force of living beings, but if I had to guess, it can only target one at a time."

She nodded slowly. "That's why it only killed one person despite being in a crowd of almost thirty."

"Yeah, it must need to feed on people every few days," I said. "What I'd like to know is how it got to Littlewood. It might have been following Parker, but since we can't ask him, Esther is the only option left."

Allie sucked in a breath. "I don't think she has any awareness of the real cause of her husband's death, Maura. It strikes me that it's far more likely that they were both in the wrong place at the wrong time."

"If I talk to her, I'm not going to *tell* her it was a demon," I clarified. "But it's possible Parker dropped a clue or two when they arranged their interview that might help me find the summoner. I'll see what Drew thinks first."

Drew had point-blank refused to help her, but her ongoing persistence meant she'd likely go back to the police again at some point. Was it proof of her own guilt, though? I didn't know.

The first customers began to trickle into the restaurant, so I went to help Jia serve them. Several wanted to ask questions about the evening's ghost tour, and we even picked up a couple of extra bookings in the process. If not for Esther's lingering threats and the prospect of another chat with her, I'd almost have begun to look forward to the evening.

Drew showed up shortly before my lunch break started, and Jia offered to take over at the bar so I could meet him outside.

"Sorry I didn't answer your message," he said. "The office is manic today, so I figured it was easier to come and talk to you in person. How's it going?"

"Great, except that Esther called Allie and started threatening her again," I said. "Have you heard from her since the last time?"

"No, I haven't." Concern laced his expression. "I suppose she decided to focus her attention elsewhere. I didn't see any interviews with her pop up in any of the local online newspapers."

"She might have gone with someone more niche," I said. "Like another ghost blogger. Do the other officers know what she's doing?"

"Not all of it," he said. "That said, I'll be in a tricky position if she does come back to request we take action again. As the head of the police force, I always have the final say, but my colleagues are already starting to question if we ought to hear her out."

"Oh boy." I guessed I shouldn't be surprised, since I hadn't exactly had the best of experiences with some of his fellow officers, and not all of them would leap to my defence if they found out that Esther's objective was to sink the inn. "You did tell them that she's being utterly irrational, right?"

"Yes, but having to keep them from finding out that I suspect any of Esther's claims have merit has put me in a difficult position."

I grimaced. That was my fault, really, but Drew was my sole supporter on the police force and likely the only reason Esther *hadn't* managed to get the other officers to hear out her claims. "It'd be easier if they had any level of trust in me."

A few weeks ago, the police and I had got into a spat when they'd arrested an innocent man on flimsy evidence behind Drew's back when the actual perpetrator was a ghost. The lengths to which certain people would go to avoid admitting they were in over their heads when it came to dealing with ghosts would have been admirable if they hadn't been so irritating.

"I'm trying." Drew took my hand. "If it helps, *I* trust you."

"You probably shouldn't." So far, for all the poking around I'd done, I hadn't unearthed anything but a stack of questions. "What did you tell them?"

"I told them Esther is acting upon paranoia alone, and since they're no more able to see ghosts than I am, they're prepared to accept that as truth."

"Good." At least they trusted *him*, or most of them did. That was the problem with involving the regular authorities in cases in which the perpetrators were already dead. Either they looked the other way, or they were forced to accept the help of an outsider who *could* see the ghosts in question.

"Your name didn't come up, don't worry," he added.

"They do know about Parker's death, but only in passing, since he's not local to the town."

"No, but it's a pain," I said. "I know it might have backfired, but if I'd been able to intercept his interview with Esther, I might have got a clue about who actually summoned that creature."

"What creature?" he asked. "It's not a ghost?"

"More of a relation." I backtracked to fill him in on my discussion with the Reaper earlier. After I'd finished, I added, "Anyway, we have another ghost tour tonight, and I'd prefer to know we aren't going to have any more disembodied unwanted guests."

Drew considered this. "You think the demon came with someone on the last tour? They weren't summoned in Hawkwood Hollow?"

"Looks that way," I said. "Parker's my main suspect at the moment, given his history of antagonising the dead, but since he's joined them in the afterlife, Esther is the only person who might be able to drop any clues."

His brows shot up. "You *want* to talk to her?"

"I don't see another option, to be honest," I said. "Everyone else who might know is either dead or unreachable. Allie isn't a fan of the idea either, but it's that or wait for her to show up here first. Esther might have been the last person to talk to Parker when he was alive."

"You don't think she's the one who set the demon on him?" he queried. "No... that would mean she killed her own husband."

"I have a hard time seeing her as the summoner," I acknowledged. "But ghosts rarely pick their targets for no reason. Same with demons."

Granted, Jonas and Esther had been part of a crowd, but Parker hadn't been, so the chances of him being picked by accident were slim. If he'd summoned the creature in the first place, it made perfect sense for it to then turn against him.

And if I was right, Esther might still be on the demon's radar herself.

"I don't know that you need to invite more trouble to your doorstep, Maura," said Drew.

"No, but we have an invisible serial killer out there and nobody remotely qualified to deal with it." *Except me.*

Drew's eyes narrowed a little as if he'd picked up on my thoughts. "There must be someone who can."

"If so, then they don't even *know* that there's a demon out there," I said. "Nobody does, except possibly Esther herself. Or Parker's friends, perhaps, but I don't know anything about them. Was he at home when he died?"

"Yes," said Drew. "His housemate found him dead in his room and called an ambulance, but it was too late. I don't think anyone was ever suspicious that his death was a result of anything other than natural causes."

"The guy made a living from ticking off ghosts," I said. "You'd think someone would have considered the possibility that one day he'd cross the wrong spirit."

Or summon it, as the case may be.

"Possibly," he said. "I don't know how much his family and friends knew about his career, but I doubt the local authorities would appreciate it if I marched in and started asking questions."

"Figures." I might have tried it myself, but I needed to know the actual address first, and I also needed to figure out if it was worth putting myself in the line of fire. Esther, at least, I could talk to on the phone from a distance. "What would you do in my place?"

"If you really want to call Esther, then make sure you have a script to follow," he said. "And ensure she doesn't realise you're probing her for information. Not that I'm supposed to encourage this."

"You could say you can offer her a last chance to say goodbye to her husband," Mart suggested from behind me.

"Definitely not." To Drew, I added, "Mart thinks I should offer to contact Jonas's ghost, but we already know he isn't reachable even if she doesn't know herself. Also, she might not yet know I'm a Reaper, if she didn't read Parker's blog."

"Yes, and that's why it's a bad idea to draw attention to yourself."

I knew Esther was nothing but trouble, but had she and her husband been directly involved in summoning the demon, or were they unlucky bystanders?

"It's only a matter of time before she shows up again," I insisted. "I won't tell her I'm a Reaper. I can claim to be acting as an employee of the inn."

"Then maybe say you're contacting her in regards to her request for compensation?" Drew suggested.

"That's an idea," said Mart. "Tie her up with paperwork so she forgets to bother you."

"I guess I can work from that," I acknowledged. "It might be too risky to try another route."

I'd have to delicately step towards the real questions without her suspecting, which would be tricky, but Drew's suggestion to write a script was a starting point.

"Sorry I couldn't be of more help," he said.

"No, it's fine," I insisted. "You've done enough, and I know you're in a bind with your fellow officers. Don't do anything that might jeopardise your own position."

"I'm not the one in danger of losing my business... or my life." His expression shadowed. "This demon..."

"It can't kill me," I told him. "Reapers are immune. Including half-Reapers, I assume, so it's no danger to me."

"Still," he said. "I'll see you later, okay? Let me know how it goes, if you do decide to call her."

"Sure." I hugged him. "Thanks anyway, Drew."

I hadn't expected him to be able to take time away from his job to help me deal with this situation, not when he was in a precarious position already. I returned to Jia, who reluctantly agreed to help me put together a script to use when I called Esther. Mart, of course, contributed with his own unhelpful suggestions of insults and jokes.

During a lull between customers and before Carey got home, I went to ask Allie for Esther's number and explained my new plan.

"You really want to call her?" she queried. "I suppose the subject of compensation might be enough to get her attention, but I already refunded her room, and I don't know that we can spare much more."

"I can pretend to be in charge of customer complaints and say to contact me instead of you in future if she has any further questions," I said. "You know how much she likes hearing herself talk. She won't be able to resist."

And if she got too persistent, I could just turn off my phone and let her shout into the void.

"I suppose." Allie handed me a piece of paper with Esther's number on it. "Just… try not to say anything that'll get either of us into even more trouble than we already are. That might be a tall order, I know, since she's looking for a fight."

"I'll do my best to stick to the script." I returned to the restaurant, where Jia gave me a thumbs-up of encouragement. *Here goes nothing.*

Holding the script I'd scrawled on a notepad in front of me, I called Esther's number and summoned up the public persona I'd used for the brief time I'd worked in a call centre. I only hoped this call wouldn't end quite as badly as that had.

"Esther Wrigley speaking," she answered. "Who is this?"

"Hey, there," I said. "I'm Maura, from the Riverside Inn Customer Relations Department. We briefly met on Friday—"

"You have a Customer Relations Department?" she said. "What a joke. Your whole business is atrocious. My husband died because of your neglect."

She spoke without pausing to breathe, making it nigh on impossible to get a word in edgeways. The script in front of me seemed inadequate in the face of her relentless ranting, so I let her ramble while I figured out how to sidestep into the right subject without angering her even further.

"I'm sorry for your loss," I said when she finally stopped to breathe. "That's why I'm calling. As I'm in charge of customer relations at the Riverside Inn, I'll be the one you can direct your complaints to in future."

"What does that mean?"

"We have a procedure for complaints, and it'll make it easier for both of us if I have the information in writing." I was pretty much improvising by this point, as I had zero intention of taking any notes whatsoever. "I need your name, your husband's name, date of birth, health conditions—"

"The cheek of it," she said. "I see what you're trying to do. My husband was perfectly healthy, so if you think you can blame his untimely death on a made-up condition, you're mistaken."

"I never suggested such a thing," I said. "I was under the impression that most life insurance policies required this kind of information. You can start by giving me the exact details of your complaint if you prefer."

"My complaint?" she said. "My husband died due to your terrible business policies—"

"How, precisely?" I spoke over her. "You've claimed both that it's our neglect that was responsible for his death and that a ghost killed him. Those are two completely different accusations."

She let out a sound like a cat whose tail had been stepped on. "I won't have you make a mockery of me."

"I need to have a statement in writing, Mrs Wrigley," I said. "What exactly do you think happened on Friday evening?"

"My husband died due to your neglect—"

It was like talking to a brick wall. I caught Jia's eye, and she shrugged, no doubt able to hear Esther's ranting even from the other side of the bar.

"Mrs Wrigley," I said impatiently. "Do you or do you not believe your husband was murdered by a ghost?"

She scoffed. "Haven't you been listening to me?"

"Yes, but if you want to pursue action against the person responsible, then we need to know who that is."

"You!" she spat. "You're responsible, all of you."

"Including the ghosts?" I'd gone far off script by this point, but there was no stopping her now. She was likely to talk until I dropped into a catatonic state from sheer exasperation, so my sole remaining option was to be as blunt as possible in the hopes that she'd drop one piece of useful information amid her spluttering.

"What?" she snapped. "Yes, of course the ghosts are responsible."

"Then why haven't you contacted someone with experience dealing with incorporeal criminals?" I queried. "No police force has the authority to arrest a ghost, and according to the law, spirits are incapable of committing murder. That would make it very difficult for anyone to be prosecuted, as there would be no guilty party."

"You're making no sense," she growled. "My husband was frightened to death by a ghost. There's no ambiguity."

"But that would mean the fault lies with the ghost in

question, wouldn't it?"

"You are guilty of endangering us both!" She screamed the words down the phone. "You and everyone associated with you will pay for this. You might have the local authorities in your pocket, but I *will* find justice, one way or another."

The call ended. I drew in a breath and looked up at a wide-eyed Jia—and Allie, who'd entered the restaurant through the automatic doors behind me.

"That went well, then?" Jia asked.

"Well... I don't think she knows about the demon." That or she was a master actress, which was possible but not likely. "I ought to have gone with a subtler approach, probably, but she's beyond ridiculous."

"She doesn't know?" Allie asked warily. "Are you sure?"

"She seems adamant that her husband was scared to death, not outright murdered, but she didn't seem to appreciate me pointing out the distinction," I said. "I was telling the truth, though—she can't prosecute a ghost."

"She *can* claim we were negligent, though," Allie said. "I didn't hear you mention Parker..."

I swore and ripped the page with the script from the notepad, tearing it in two. "Too late for that. She had a one-track mind."

"She might have already forgotten him," said Jia. "He was her outlet for her to publish her rage, nothing more."

"Lovely woman." I scowled. "Tell you what, it'd be the twist of the century if it turns out *she* killed her own husband after all."

"For what reason?" Allie asked. "To sink our business? She'd never been to Hawkwood Hollow before, as far as I know, and I'd never set eyes on her before last week."

"Maybe I should have asked where she heard of our tour company," I said. "I was too concerned with finding out if she knew about the demon, even if she didn't summon it herself."

"Who do you think did summon it, then—Parker?" asked Allie. "No… the demon wouldn't have turned against the person who summoned it."

"It's actually pretty common for that to happen," I said. "They often either turn on the person who summoned them or attack innocent bystanders instead of the actual target. Demons can take orders, but that doesn't mean they'll listen to someone they deem inferior."

Especially amateur ghost hunters with inflated egos.

"If it's true, then is there anyone else who might have been in contact with Parker?" asked Allie.

"He had housemates, Drew said," I replied. "The trouble is, Drew's hands are tied. He's the only person who can stop his fellow officers from deciding to give Esther an audience. He probably has Parker's address, but he'll get into trouble if he goes looking on my behalf."

"Yeah, that's tricky," said Allie. "Best to put it out of mind today and focus on this evening's tour instead. Don't let Carey know you spoke to Esther either."

"Wise idea." That would just distract her from the upcoming tour, which was a scant few hours away. Though my conversation with Esther had made me wonder if we shouldn't have cancelled after all in case the demon came back.

Whoever the summoner was, the demon's current location was the question that ought to worry us. Having taken out Parker, would it remain in Littlewood, or might it come back to Hawkwood Hollow?

Don't be absurd, Maura, I told myself. Even if I turned out to be right, a murdering spirit wouldn't let a cancelled event prevent it from coming back to the inn. All we'd do is dig ourselves a financial hole and leave a trail of disgruntled customers behind us. And Esther wouldn't actually show up at the inn that evening… right?

11

B y the time Carey came home from school, my nerves were already on edge, and even Mart wasn't his usual boisterous self. Jia seemed twitchy, too, though she promised to help me keep an eye out for any ghosts that didn't belong without startling the guests. A couple of hours before the tour's starting time, we gave the whole inn a thorough search while Allie took over serving at the restaurant. I used my Reaper ability to peer into the afterworld at every corner, but nothing caught my attention.

When we came downstairs, we found Carey nervously hovering at the table nearest to the bar. She'd changed out of her school uniform and into her best cloak and hat, but she lacked the confident anticipation of her first tour night.

"Are you sure we should be doing this?" she whispered to Jia and me.

"Bit late to cancel now," I remarked in a low voice, having seen that a handful of people had already gathered in the lobby to wait for the tour to kick off. "Jia and I didn't see any signs of trouble, but if there is, then we'll take care of it."

"Sure thing," said Jia. "If anyone comes in here who shouldn't—living or dead—then we'll give them the boot."

That included Esther, though we hadn't heard from her since her temper tantrum earlier. It was probably too much to hope that I'd successfully irritated her into leaving us alone. She'd certainly be back, but not tonight—I hoped.

"Have you searched the entire inn?" Carey asked. "Every single room?"

"Not all the guests' rooms." Maybe I should have, but that would involve a lot of awkward questions and the chance of everyone being exposed to my Reaper status if I had to use my shadow-walking abilities. Besides, we didn't need to give our guests any reason to suspect that we were on the lookout for further trouble. "Relax, it'll be fine. Do you have the health and safety forms ready?"

"Yes." Allie stepped out from behind the bar, and Jia took her place. "I might as well ask the people in the lobby to fill them out early, to save time later."

A steady trickle of guests showed up over the course of the next hour, some to check in at the inn and some here solely for the tour. Nobody raised a fuss over being asked to sign a health and safety form, though there were a few whispers and raised eyebrows when Drew entered the lobby shortly before the tour was due to start.

I met him at the door. "Thanks for coming."

"No problem at all," he murmured. "Everything okay?"

"So far, yes." I scanned the lobby, seeing mostly unfamiliar faces among the crowd. Nobody was taking photos this time around, as far as I could tell, but I remained tense as Carey stepped to the front with the microphone in hand to address the crowd. Jia took up a position on the opposite side of the lobby, while Mart hovered beside the restaurant door. Alone. Wait, that wasn't right.

Surreptitiously, I edged closer to my brother and dropped my voice. "Where are the other ghosts?"

"I don't know. I thought you did."

"No..." I'd been so busy keeping an eye out for trouble that I'd somehow missed that every ghost except for Mart was no longer downstairs. I didn't see them in the restaurant *or* the lobby. Oh boy.

"Maura." Drew edged over to me, finding it considerably harder to move stealthily than I did—not just because he was taller and broader than me, but because his status and reputation as the head of the police attracted whispers and glances wherever he walked.

"It's okay," I mouthed at him. "I'll handle it."

He halted, his expression not entirely convinced, but he nodded and returned to his former position watching the doors. Meanwhile, I turned to Jia and frantically signalled for her to move closer.

Jia leaned over and whispered, "What is it?"

"Can you see any ghosts in here, except my brother?"

"No." Her eyes widened. "Wait, they're not here?"

"Apparently not." Had they all got stage fright at the same time? I gave the crowd another urgent scan in case one of them was hiding at the back, but I didn't dare go full Reaper in public, which left me with my inadequate regular human senses. I might have ducked outside to check the afterworld, but that would involve leaving Carey and the others vulnerable. I didn't dare take the risk.

I held out until Carey finished her speech. An anticipatory silence followed her announcement of the tour's start, punctured by ripples of confusion when the ghosts didn't burst into the lobby as they were supposed to. Carey gave me a quizzical look, and Jia cleared her throat and addressed the crowd. "Erm, it looks like the ghosts are taking a nap. Perhaps we can wake them up if we make enough noise?"

As she corralled the crowd into polite applause, I raised my brows at Mart, signalling to him to come to our rescue. He gave a dramatic sigh, and then the lights flickered and went out. The tour group laughed, assuming it was part of the act, and as the applause turned genuine, some of the tension melted a little.

While Mart kept the crowd's attention, I seized on the chance to move closer to Jia. "We have to find them."

"How?" she whispered back. "Only the two of us can see them."

"I know, but—can you cover for me while I check in the afterworld?"

Not that I wanted to turn my back on the others, but I also didn't want to put a dent in Carey's confidence by telling her that our ghosts had done a runner. If Mart kept up the act, then Carey might not realise anything was amiss any more than the rest of the crowd did, but would my brother be able to fulfil the roles of five ghosts at the same time?

While the crowd began to move towards the restaurant, I waited in the lobby, debating the best place from which to search the afterworld. The games room might be a surer bet than outside, because there was always the chance of someone looking out of the window at an inopportune moment.

"Maura." Drew stepped to my side. "What's going on?"

"Aside from my brother, our ghosts have gone AWOL." I spied a free route to the games room, which I approached. "I'm going to have a look in the afterworld. Drew—you should wait out here in case anyone's counting on me being distracted to start trouble."

It was possible the spirits had left of their own accord, given their skittishness over the past few days, but I wasn't going to take any chances. While Drew waited in the lobby, I ducked into the games room. First I checked every corner, including under the pool table.

Okay. Time to use the Reaper approach, then.

Darkness spread from my hands, and I whispered, "Hey. Jonathan. Brian. Everyone. Where are you?"

No answer. Frowning, I raised my voice a little. "Vicky? Louise? Wade?"

After a long moment of silence, Vicky's transparent form became visible, crouching against the darkness of the afterworld. Lifting her head, she let out a moan and then vanished once more.

"What…?" I faltered. "Vicky?"

She appeared again, her transparent body flickering like a TV losing its signal. "I can't…"

She vanished. Baffled, I tried another name. "Jonathan?"

Another long silence followed before he popped up in the afterworld, his body curled in a defensive position.

"Hey—Jonathan," I called to him. "What's wrong?"

"I can't—" He cringed, arms over his head. "I can't come back in."

Then his ghostly form flickered out of existence, just like Vicky's had. *Can't come back in? Meaning the inn?*

Now thoroughly rattled, I backed out of the games room and crossed the lobby to the door, near which Drew stood.

"You're not leaving, are you?" he asked.

"I'm going to check outside the inn," I told him. "The ghosts say they can't come back in, so I need to find out why. It won't take long."

The sound of Carey's voice addressing the crowd from the restaurant followed me out through the automatic doors. Hoping she'd captured their attention enough that they wouldn't see me leaving, I walked around the inn's right-hand side and called for the missing ghosts again.

"Vicky? Jonathan?"

Once again, their transparent forms materialised against the shadows of the afterworld, hunched over as if in pain.

"What's wrong?" I asked. "Seriously—where is everyone?"

"We can't come in," Jonathan said. "There's something inside the inn keeping us from entering."

"What?" My heart lurched. "Mart's inside the inn. He's fine."

I think. I was already walking back towards the inn's entrance to check, just as Mart himself came drifting into view. He floated through the closed doors and halted in front of me, crossing his arms over his chest. "Thought you could sneak off, did you? You owe me majorly for making me run a tour all by myself, you know."

"I'll make it up to you later," I told him. "The other ghosts are saying something's wrong at the inn and they can't come inside."

The doors slid open as Allie approached from the lobby. "Maura, is something wrong?"

"The ghosts have left the inn," I explained. "Except Mart. I don't know why, but they seem to think there's something inside the inn keeping them out."

"I don't see any problems," Mart put in. "I think they're slacking off. Should I go and berate them?"

"Not until after the tour," I told him. "Allie—try to keep everything going as normal, and don't tell Carey. I'll find whatever the problem is and deal with it."

"All right." Concern flickered across her expression, but she left the lobby and returned to the restaurant to join her daughter.

Had Jia and I somehow missed something huge in our search of the inn? I'd never thought ghosts *not* being around would be the issue of the night, but Mart grew more and more visibly impatient as the evening progressed and the source of the other ghosts' absence failed to materialise.

While Carey led the guests upstairs for the next part of the tour, Mart kept up a steady stream of complaints as he drifted alongside me at the rear of their group.

"I'm exhausted," he whined at me. "I've never worked this hard in my life."

"So am I, and I actually need sleep, unlike you," I muttered. "Look, there isn't long before the tour's done, and you'll get a huge round of applause at the end. You can hold out until then, can't you?"

When we reached the top of the stairs, Mart jerked to a stop as if he'd run into a solid wall. "What... ow!"

"What is it?" I lowered my voice when a couple of the people at the back of the crowd glanced over their shoulders.

Mart didn't answer, but I hadn't seen him look this horrified since the last time he'd come face-to-face with a zombie.

"Mart?"

"I have to go."

He spun on his heel and fled downstairs, leaving me alone at the far end of the corridor. Blinking in confusion, I watched Jia make her way through the crowd to join me.

"Where'd Mart go?" she asked in an undertone.

"He ran downstairs," I murmured back. "I don't have a clue why, but it was like he hit an invisible wall when he came up here."

I retreated to the part of the corridor where he'd been stopped in his tracks, but I didn't see or sense anything that might have tripped up a ghost, and I couldn't exactly peer into the afterworld with a bunch of strangers crowding the corridor in front of me.

I was tempted to ask Carey to immediately get everyone downstairs, but she was on the other side of the crowd, who'd begun to stir with impatience again. *Ack. Mart's not keeping them entertained any longer.* While he'd be able to make noise from downstairs, that wouldn't be nearly as impactful.

A solution popped into my mind, but it would involve some sleight of hand on my behalf. "Jia, can you help Carey handle the crowd? I'm going to take over from Mart."

"Sure." Her eyes widened a little when she realised what I meant, but she didn't argue with my plan. While Jia got to work helping Carey to keep the crowd occupied, I backed out of the corridor and down the stairs.

Once I was certain nobody could see me, I prepared to put on a show. Shadows flooded the area around my feet, and I stepped into the dark, emerging on the other side of the upstairs corridor. Stealthily, I flicked off the nearest light switch and then hopped into the shadows again.

Delighted laughter came from the crowd as they realised they were being haunted again, while I emerged behind the closed door of my room. It was a good job I had a thorough memory of the layout of the upper floor of the inn, because I'd have to tread carefully to avoid being caught in the act. I crossed my room on swift feet and closed the bathroom door loudly enough for the crowd to hear. I hopped in and out of the neighbouring vacant rooms one at a time, slamming doors inside each one. It wasn't quite as dramatic as making the temperature drop or grabbing anyone's hands from behind, but it certainly did the job.

When I emerged from the shadows near the stairs, a strange smell lingered in the air. Wait, I knew that smell… sage. Where had I picked that up?

Is that what sent the ghosts away? I sniffed again, trying to pick up the smell's location, but it might have come from any of the rooms I'd jumped in and out of, and I wouldn't be able to conduct a proper search until the crowd was back downstairs.

I finished the show with a dramatic rattling of all the doors in the upper corridor, to applause. Then I waited for the thunder of footsteps downstairs to fade before I resumed my search for the elusive smell. The scent of sage became more distinct now the crowd had moved downstairs, and I followed it to a door.

The room was unoccupied, so I entered without needing to knock. The smell grew noticeably stronger, and I followed it to the source: a line of herbs sprinkled on the carpeted floor. Sage, and others that I hazarded a guess were used for similar purposes. Namely, as a ghost repellent.

No guests were currently staying in this room, but Allie used thorough cleaning spells after every guest left the inn. Which meant someone had sneaked in and left a ghost-repelling charm at some point in the past day.

I closed the door and jogged to the stairs, where I found a concerned-looking Drew peering up at me from the lobby. "I wondered where you'd gone."

"Someone put sage and some other herbs in one of the empty rooms," I whispered. "That must have scared off the ghosts."

It was better than our tour being infiltrated by murderous spirits, but who'd been responsible? I couldn't walk in front of the crowd and ask without publicly admitting we'd lost all our ghosts and that I'd been duping them, and the odds of a public confession were as unlikely as Esther having a sudden change of heart.

"Scared them off?" Drew's brows rose. "Can I help?"

"Yeah—can you make sure nobody comes upstairs while I deal with this?"

"Sure thing," he said. "If I see Allie or Jia, should I tell them?"

"Yeah, why not." I needed to find out who'd previously occupied the room, though it was equally likely that some opportunistic person had slipped in when nobody was paying attention—seemingly for the sole purpose of driving away our ghosts and wrecking the tour.

I ran back upstairs and grabbed an empty bag from my room before heading to the scene of the crime. The smell was even more obvious from the corridor without any guests present, and it was no wonder the other ghosts had run off. Strange that Mart hadn't noticed from downstairs, but perhaps he'd built up more of a tolerance from spending so much time around me.

After scooping the herbs off the carpet and into the bag, I went back downstairs to join Drew.

He tilted his head. "Everything okay?"

I showed him the bag. "I'm gonna have to get rid of these if I want the ghosts to come back in."

Applause drifted through the transparent doors to the restaurant as Carey gave the last part of her tour speech. While everyone's attention was on her, I seized the chance to run outside and went to dump the herbs in the river. While the fast-flowing water carried them away, I returned to the inn.

Mart recoiled from me in the lobby. "What's that smell?"

"That's what stopped you from getting upstairs," I told him. "Someone gathered a bunch of ghost-repelling herbs and dumped them in an empty room. I threw them in the river, so you should be fine now."

"I can still smell them on you," Mart said accusingly.

"I'll have a shower later." I turned to Drew. "No trouble in here?"

"No, but I think Jia is getting a bit impatient."

I headed for the restaurant and had to sidestep several people leaving; Jia must have talked Carey into finishing the tour in there instead of the lobby like the last time. I'd have to wait for the guests to depart for their rooms before I called the ghosts back, so I waited in the lobby for Jia and Allie to return.

When they did, Allie made a beeline for me. "Maura, is everything okay? Did you find out what the problem was?"

"Someone put a ghost-proofing spell in one of the empty rooms," I told her and Jia in a low voice. "Do you know who the last person was who stayed in the second room to the right of mine, opposite the stairs?"

"Yes." Her eyes widened. "The last guests to stay in there were Esther and her husband."

Jia swore under her breath. "Seriously?"

"Did they actually stay there, though?" I asked. "Wait—it can't have been Esther. The ghosts were fine yesterday, and she hasn't been back since Saturday."

"Someone might have unlocked the door and gone inside," Allie said. "I didn't check after I cleaned the room over the weekend. I should have."

"You couldn't have expected someone to break into the room for the sole purpose of disrupting our tour," said Jia. "Did you get rid of the spell, Maura?"

"Yeah, I threw it in the river." I watched the crowd dispersing from the restaurant, though some people lingered behind to ask Carey questions. "Might take the ghosts a bit longer to come back, though."

After most of the guests had left—either to return to their rooms or to go home, if they weren't staying in Hawkwood Hollow—Carey came bounding over to our corner of the lobby.

"Hey," she said to us. "That went better than I expected. I don't think the guests were as excited as the ones on the first night, but nothing's wrong, is it? I noticed the ghosts weren't as active as usual."

"Someone left a ghost-repelling spell upstairs," I explained. "It drove all the spirits out of the inn except for Mart."

"Seriously?" Her face fell. "Why not tell me?"

126

"I knew trying to explain it in front of the tour participants would just complicate things and distract you," I said. "I got rid of the spell, so there's nothing to worry about."

Except that someone had actively tried to sabotage our tour, and if it hadn't been Esther, then who might it have been?

12

The following day, I woke up utterly unrested and without much of a plan for my next move. While the tour had undeniably been a success as far as the guests were concerned, the knowledge that someone had tried to sabotage us by driving away our ghosts weighed on my mind, as did the question of who it might be. The previous night, Jia and I had spent nearly an hour coaxing the missing spirits back to the inn, not at all helped by Mart, who'd decided that he'd already done more than his fair share of good deeds and had gone back to hiding in the games room.

If it hadn't been Esther herself who'd put those herbs in her room, which was unlikely, then any of our current and previous guests of the past few days was a possible contender. If I called Esther again, she'd be justified in telling me to get lost, so I was left with little choice but to look to the other guests for answers.

I avoided mentioning the subject until after Carey had left for school, at which point Mart cornered me in the lobby. "We need to talk about my payment for yesterday. You owe me for making me run that tour single-handedly."

I groaned under my breath. "You get to pick the movie for the next few weeks?"

"Not good enough," he said. "The other ghosts will go on strike if you don't let any of them have a turn at picking the film, besides. Come on, you can think of something better than that."

Honestly. "You can have the day off. The week off."

"I want more."

"Like what?" I was out of ideas, not at all helped by my lack of decent sleep. "I already let you use my shower when I'm not around, despite you flooding my room at least once a week."

"I only did that twice," he said indignantly.

"Then by all means come up with a list of demands and bring them to me later," I said to him. "I need to find whoever tried to ghost-proof the inn, preferably before they try again. You wouldn't like that, would you?"

"You're trying to distract me."

"No, I'm trying to stop you from getting banished," I told him. "Also, you've had nothing but glowing compliments from everyone who was on the tour, so I don't know what you're complaining about."

"Compliments won't pay the bills."

"You don't have any bills to pay."

When he huffed and floated away with his nose in the air, Allie cleared her throat from behind the desk. "Talking to your brother?"

"Yeah, he's peeved that I made him work for free yesterday," I explained. "I didn't really have a choice. We don't have a backup team."

Though considering the ghost-proof spell would have

affected any spirit in the vicinity, having spare ghosts on our team wouldn't have helped us either.

"The ghosts came back, right?" she asked.

"They did," I confirmed. "But if we can't confirm who was responsible for putting that ghost-repellent upstairs, then there's a chance we might have a repeat performance at Friday's tour. I'm pretty sure it wasn't Esther, despite the spell being in her room."

"Who else would have done such a thing, though?"

"I don't know. I'd say Parker, but he's dead."

Sofia's face came to mind. She'd certainly had good reason to sabotage us, and she'd rubbed me up the wrong way even before I'd learned she was an ex-coven member. She'd left town, but she'd had ample time to sneak into Esther's room since her arrival when nobody was watching her. How to prove it, though, when she was no longer here?

Well… if she'd been in touch with any of the coven's current members, they might know. Especially if the herbs she'd used to make her anti-ghost spell had been locally purchased.

The doors slid open, and Jia entered the lobby, greeting both of us with a tired wave. "How's it going?"

I gave a noncommittal shrug. "I just came up with a theory. What if those herbs in Esther's room came from the coven's supplies? Might it be worth checking if any of them saw who took them?"

"I guess." She glanced over at Allie, who was frowning at her computer screen and hadn't heard us. "We should have time to run over there before opening time."

"Good call." I walked over to the desk. "Hey, Allie. Can Jia and I drop by the coven's headquarters to see if they know if anyone bought or borrowed any ghost-proofing herbs in the past few days?"

"Sure," she said without looking up. "As long as you're back in time to start your shift."

"Don't worry, we will be."

We left the inn, and when the doors closed behind us, I turned to Jia. "What was that about?"

"I think she was reading reviews of the inn and our ghost tours."

"Oh boy." I didn't blame her for wanting to get a feel for the general feedback we were getting. At least nobody had dropped dead during yesterday's tour, which was a hell of a low bar. As for the most recent act of sabotage, Jia and I would ensure there wouldn't be a repeat performance.

We walked across the bridge to the high street, where the coven's headquarters were located. The squat brick building stood out among its neighbours due to its magenta hue and the murals of mythical creatures painted on the walls, which remained from Mina Devlin's days as coven leader. The automatic doors slid open to let us enter, and I was thoroughly unsurprised when the sole witch in the lobby reacted to our appearance with a loud gasp. "Reaper, what are you doing here?"

Wendy, a rail-thin witch with an irritating habit of wringing her hands constantly as if distressed at the world in general, came running downstairs as if she had an alarm strapped to her wrist that went off whenever anyone said the word 'Reaper.'

"Why are you here?" Wendy asked. "You can't possibly need supplies again already."

Already? She was watching the other day, was she? "I just came to ask a question. Is Jennifer in?"

"She's busy," she evaded. "You can't keep coming in here. It's bad for business."

"What business?" Jia said. "You're not selling anything."

True. If anything, the coven was a charity, funded entirely by its own members, and if Sofia had snagged the herbs she'd used from here, she'd technically stolen the coven's property.

"We have a reputation to uphold," Wendy said haughtily. "People are concerned about the Reaper wandering in and out whenever she feels like."

"Your own leader said I could come back at any time," I pointed out. "Since I'm a witch as much as I am a Reaper, it's within my rights to. All I wanted to know is if anyone's taken any supplies to make a ghost-proof spell recently."

She gave me an odd look. "Why on earth would you want to know that?"

"Because someone decided to try to sabotage our ghost-tour business by setting up a concoction to scare off the spirits."

Her mouth parted. "So you assume it was someone in the coven?"

"We had an ex-coven member staying at the inn." Jia stepped in. "Sofia Granger. You know her?"

Wendy shook her head fiercely. "No, I most certainly do not."

"You sure about that?" I squinted at her face, but it was beyond me to tell if her hand-wringing was due to guilt or just her natural state. "Does Jennifer know?"

"Jennifer would never allow an ex-coven member to come in here." She drew in a steadying breath. "That's why you both have to leave."

Would Jennifer have noticed Sofia paying a visit? Wendy certainly would have, and while her honesty was questionable, I didn't believe she would open the doors to any of Mina Devlin's cronies.

"Fine," I said. "As long as you're telling the truth."

There was nothing to do if she wasn't, but Jennifer had no reason to want to sabotage our business *or* help Mina

Devlin in any capacity, and neither did her overeager assistant.

When Jia and I returned to the inn, we found Allie in the same spot as before, her eyes fixed on her computer screen.

"You're not still reading the inn's reviews, are you?" I walked over to the desk. "What's up?"

"Maura, look at this." She showed me her computer screen. "See the name on this review?"

The review was posted on the inn's website... and the name attached to it was Parker Maven.

"What's going on?" asked Jia.

"We seem to have got a review from a dead guy." I stepped back to let her see the screen too.

"Is someone else using his name?" Jia suggested. "Weird."

Belatedly, I remembered Mart had access to Parker's email address, but however much I'd annoyed him yesterday, I didn't see him going so far as to leave us a negative review in someone else's name. Besides, he'd have had to use my computer or phone in order to do so. "Has anyone checked his blog since the last time?"

"No." Jia pulled out her phone, while I went in search of Mart.

My brother wasn't in the games room, so I walked through the doors into the restaurant and spied him lurking behind the bar.

"Mart." I beckoned to him. "Come over here."

"What now?" He scowled at me. "I thought you wanted me to write you a list of demands. If you have another urgent situation you need my help with, I'm fully booked for another thirty years."

"Parker seems to have left a review on our website," I told him. "Does that sound likely to you?"

"That's not all." Jia came running into the restaurant behind me. "The review post on his blog is back up."

"Seriously?" I whipped around to see her phone screen, and sure enough, the topmost review on Parker's blog once again showed a photo of our inn. "How is that possible?"

"No clue." Her brow wrinkled. "Is he haunting a computer somewhere, do you think?"

"I doubt it." Though her comment reminded me that I hadn't tried to contact his ghost. I'd been working under the assumption that he had met the same fate as Jonas's spirit, but who else could have revived his blog post from the literal dead?

"He wasn't on the tour yesterday," said Mart. "No ghosts were, except for me."

"I know." I reached for my phone. "Can you take down the post again? Please?"

He pouted. "What am I, your personal servant?"

"That's not... fine, I'll do it myself." I'd change the password while I was at it, which I should have asked Mart to do from the start. *What a nuisance.*

While I loaded up Parker's website on my phone, Jia said, "The restaurant opens in ten minutes. If you want to chat to his ghost, now might be the time to do it."

"Yeah... it'd be easier for me to find him near the place where he died, but I have enough herbs to use a summoning spell if necessary."

"Yeah." She glanced towards the door. "Do it outside. I'll take over here."

"Cheers." I jogged upstairs to my room to fetch my bag of supplies before heading to my usual ghost-summoning spot near the river.

Once out of sight of the inn, I tapped into my Reaper powers to summon the afterworld. Dark shadows flooded the area around me, and I called out Parker's name.

"Parker Maven," I said to the darkness. "I want to talk to you."

No answer came. My jaw twitched, though I should have known better than to expect an instant response. When he didn't reply to his name, I reached into the bag of herbs and began laying them out until an unbroken circle surrounded me.

"Parker," I called into the circle. "I summon you. Parker."

Yet again, there was no reply.

"Parker Maven, answer me, you conniving menace. If you're going to lie about me from the afterlife, then at least have the guts to come back and explain yourself."

"No luck," Mart said, having followed me. "Guess he moved on."

"Like Jonas." Frustration burned under my skin. "Then who's pretending to be him online?"

Someone who didn't think much of us, evidently, but I didn't get it at all. If all the recent events had been someone's elaborate scheme to sink our business, then surely Parker's death hadn't been part of the plan. And just where was the demonic spirit hiding? I could theoretically have used a summoning spell to draw it here if it was close enough, but not all afterworld beasts were frightened off by the presence of sage, and I didn't dare risk the others' safety. While Reapers might be immune to their powers, there were other targets in the area—like Jia, Carey, or Allie. The mere thought made me shudder, so I dismantled the summoning spell, kicked the herbs into the river, and returned to the inn.

"No luck?" Jia guessed when I joined her behind the counter.

"It was a long shot." I heaved a sigh and picked up my phone. "This is ridiculous. You'd think the whole universe was out to stop us from running a successful business."

I was just loading up Parker's blog when the restaurant door opened and three people walked in. Esther strode in the lead, and behind her were two alarmingly huge individuals

135

with grey skin and tusks. *Ogres.* What had she done now, got herself a pair of bodyguards to fire threats at the inn? My heart sank to see her smug expression and then sank even more when she walked straight up to the bar. "This is the end for you, Reaper."

The last word echoed off the walls of the empty restaurant, and I thanked my sole remaining lucky star that no customers had shown up yet. *Reaper.* She finally knew.

"Excuse me?" I dragged my gaze from her face to the giants flanking her. *Where did they come from?*

"Yes, I know what you are," she said in triumphant tones. "You might have tried to hide your true nature, but justice always prevails."

"What are you doing here?" Allie came running in from the lobby, skidding to a halt in front of the two towering ogres. "You... who are you?"

"We're with the Wardens." The ogre on Esther's left-hand side spoke in a rumbling growl of a voice. "We're here because we have reason to believe one of your staff summoned a demon and set it loose, killing two people."

Esther bared her teeth in a grin. "You thought you could fob me off with excuses, but I found someone willing to listen to my concerns. The monster you set loose won't be allowed to kill anyone else."

"You think *I* summoned a demon?" The word *Warden* rang through my skull. She'd taken my suggestion to heart and gone directly to the Wardens—one of the few organisations that *did* have the kind of specialist skills necessary to deal with the demon.

I hadn't expected her to find them, and I sure as hell hadn't expected them to accuse *me* of doing the summoning.

"I knew it." Esther's eyes gleamed with triumph and rage in equal measures. "You thought it was funny to play me for a fool, did you? You knew what killed my husband all along."

"Look—I didn't summon anything." I racked my thoughts for any information that might help convince her and her snarly bodyguards that I wasn't the person they needed to arrest. "I talked to the local Reaper, Harold, and he suggested a demon might have been responsible for your husband's death. That's the only reason the thought even crossed my mind."

"You don't deny that you're a Reaper," growled the ogre on her right. "Do you?"

"Half-Reaper, and that doesn't make me responsible for summoning anything," I said. "Be realistic here. Why would I want her husband dead? We'd never even met before Friday, and he was a guest at the inn. We wouldn't get many bookings if we made a habit of murdering our customers, would we?"

Esther's face flushed. "You dare to make light of your own predicament? You've dug your own grave, Reaper."

Ignoring her, I addressed the ogres instead. "I'm not the person you need to arrest. You can check my room if you like, but you'll find no evidence that I summoned any demons."

Ogres couldn't see ghosts or demons any more than Esther could, but they tended to be high up in the Wardens' ranks, so they'd almost certainly know someone with that talent. Esther must have found the nearest branch of Wardens and marched straight to the top office. She was far more persistent than I'd ever have believed, and it only added insult to injury that the Wardens were more likely to be able to deal with the demon if they let me help them. Now that Esther had labelled me a suspect, she'd killed any chance I might have had of being able to find her husband's killer.

Yes, unlike the Reaper Council, the Wardens didn't have any authority over me... but they could easily report me to someone who did. *This is bad. Really bad.*

"We'll certainly be searching the premises," said the ogre on Esther's left. "Demon or no demon, a rogue Reaper is not something that we can allow to go ignored."

My mouth went dry. "I don't use my Reaper training at all. I'm not a rogue."

"You're running ghost tours, aren't you?"

Esther scoffed. "Your lies get more and more outrageous."

"A third of all witches can see ghosts," I pointed out. "Being able to *see* ghosts isn't the same as summoning them, and I'm not breaking any laws by trying to earn a living."

"You broke the law by summoning a demon," said Esther. "Don't try to weasel out of this one. I don't know or care about the Reapers' laws, but I know who killed my husband, and I know you did the same to Parker Maven too. You were scared I might expose the truth to him, weren't you?"

When the two ogres each took a step forwards, I felt the blood drain from my face. "I didn't have anything to do with Parker's death."

"You and Parker Maven had a history," growled one of the ogres. "Esther tells us that the two of you argued on the night of her husband's death and that you were upset by the review he posted on his blog."

Alarm blared through me. "He was taking photos of Jonas's body. I told him to stop, and in retaliation, he posted lies about us on his blog. That's the whole story."

"And *you* retaliated by having him killed," Esther said. "You knew we were about to have an interview and share the truth with the world, didn't you?"

"You're mistaken." My words were ineffectual, not least because if the ogres looked at my phone, they'd see for themselves that I'd visited his website recently. I *had* argued with Parker, and thanks to whoever had revived that blog post, his claims of my status as a rogue Reaper were once again on display for the world to see.

"I'm afraid we cannot believe you," said the Warden. "You, Maura Clarke, are breaking the law according to the rules of the Wardens *and* the Reaper Council. You're under arrest."

13

The ogre's words hung in the air for one interminable moment, as if time itself slowed down. Then, as they made to move towards me, the door to the restaurant flew open, and Drew came running in.

"Stop," he told the ogres. "I'm the head of the police force in Hawkwood Hollow, and you don't have the authority to come in here and arrest a citizen of our town without any cause."

I stared at him. Never mind how he'd got here so fast—how in the world had he known the ogres were here to begin with? I'd have to ask later, because Esther's fury at being interrupted was outclassed only by the hostility emanating from the two ogres. Luckily, this time their ire was directed at Drew instead of me.

"I beg to differ," growled the ogre on the left. "Maura Clarke has broken the laws of the Reapers and of the magical world as a whole, and that's reason enough to take her into custody."

"Whatever happened to innocent until proven guilty?" I found my voice. "I didn't summon any demons, and I'm not an active Reaper. In fact, if you talk to Harold, who *is* the town's active Reaper, he can confirm both of those things are true. I didn't even know it might be a demon that killed Jonas until Harold suggested it himself, and he can back me up."

"That is correct," Drew said. "I'd suggest you talk to the local Reaper before you make any rash decisions. He lives in the town's cemetery. I can give you directions if you need them."

Belatedly, I realised Drew hadn't brought backup. Had he come here alone on purpose, or had his fellow officers refused to come to my defence? I suspected the latter, though it still baffled me how he'd even known the Wardens had been threatening me in the first place.

"Rash decisions?" Esther glowered at Drew. "My husband died, and your department did nothing but dismiss my concerns and lie to me. You knew his death wasn't an accident from the start, didn't you?"

"No, we did not," I answered for Drew. "I also don't know why Parker was targeted by the same demon that killed your husband, but I haven't seen him since he left the inn."

"I can vouch for Maura, too, if need be," added Jia.

"And me," said Allie.

"Coming from her fellow conspirators, that means nothing," Esther scoffed. "Even if you have the police on your side, you won't be allowed to get away with your despicable behaviour."

Drew waited for a gap in her ranting and addressed the ogres. "The Wardens can't make arrests in this town without asking permission from the local authorities. Namely, me."

"Ah, but in this case, we can." Esther smirked. "Maura Clarke isn't local and is therefore subject to the rules of her own community, not this one."

"I am local." The thought of my original town, where I'd

grown up, sent a nasty jolt through my chest. "I haven't always lived here, but I've lived in a lot of places."

"Maura is employed by me," said Allie. "We're a local business. That makes her one of us."

"According to the laws, she belongs to the town in which her Reaper parent resides," growled the ogre on Esther's left-hand side. "That said, we did not come here to argue about semantics. If you believe the local Reaper has information to share, we'll certainly speak with him."

"Yes," said the second ogre. "We will."

Esther didn't budge. "I'm not leaving this building. If we leave the Reaper unwatched, she'll just try to escape."

"I'm not escaping anywhere, because I *live* here," I said through gritted teeth. "Unless you want me to come with you to talk to the Reaper myself so you can keep an eye on me?"

"Certainly not," answered one of the ogres. "We'll judge for ourselves if his answers to our questions are satisfactory."

"Ask Harold to give you the contact details for Shelton, another local Reaper," I told the ogres. "He's met me and verified on behalf of the Council that I'm not a practising Reaper. If you need a second opinion."

"We'll certainly look into that," rumbled one of the retreating ogres. "But if we return and find you gone, then the consequences will be on you."

The two ogres lumbered out of the restaurant, having to duck to fit their towering forms through the doorway. Drew made to follow them and then paused. "Maura, I need to tell my officers what's going on. I'll come back, okay?"

"Sure." There was more I wanted to say, but not in front of Esther, who seemed determined to stay put in case I ran off. Which was exactly the plan, because I refused to stand here and let myself be arrested for a crime I'd never committed.

As Drew left, Esther gave me a smirk, and a fresh spike of

panic ran through my nerves. With Drew's departure went a fair bit of my courage, and I didn't know if I had it in me to endure Esther's ranting for longer than a few minutes before cracking and hexing her.

"Not so full of yourself now, are you?" She gave a smug smile that encompassed me *and* Allie and Jia. Neither of them could challenge her, not without getting into trouble, but since I was screwed either way, I might as well try to knock that smirk off her face.

"What exactly do you have to gain from this?" I asked. "You already received all the compensation we could offer. If you're really interested in getting rid of that demon and preventing it from attacking anyone else, then I'm the only person who might be able to help you. Not even most of the Wardens have that skill."

It was a risk telling her that much, but my only remaining option was to convince her—or at least the Wardens—that I was better off working on their side than against them if they wanted to find the demon and send it back to the afterworld.

"Help me?" She scoffed. "You expect me to believe your claims after the number of lies you told? You even had the gall to tell me my husband's death was an accident when you were perfectly aware that it wasn't."

"That was my responsibility, and I'm sorry for that." Allie stepped in. "I can't see ghosts myself, so I believed the paramedics who examined his body when they said he died of natural causes. If you don't mind my asking, what exactly convinced you otherwise? Who did you speak to?"

What's she doing? Trying to take the attention off me, perhaps, though I was also curious as to how Esther had figured out a demon was behind the deaths. I hadn't told anyone outside of a handful of people, and I'd thought everyone else believed Parker's death was a complete accident. Old Harold couldn't have told her, which left... who?

Esther ignored her and addressed me instead. "You almost had me fooled, you know. I was starting to doubt my husband's death was the result of a ghost before my eyes were opened."

"By whom?" I interjected. "Parker Maven? I might remind you that he posted photos of your husband's body on his blog and ignored my requests to put his camera away at the scene. That's the only reason I tried to contact him again."

"Stop talking," she said. "I won't hear another one of your lies."

"I'm telling the truth." Parker might have stoked her paranoia, but he was dead, despite someone else apparently having access to his online accounts. Had they been in touch with Esther too?

I had some suspicions as to who it might be, but I couldn't do anything with Esther's watchful eye on me. Besides, I was far more concerned for the others than for myself. No regular prison cell could contain a Reaper, and while the Wardens had direct contact with the Reaper Council themselves... well, I couldn't believe I was counting on old Harold to have my back. Again.

Esther opened her mouth, presumably to begin another tirade, and her phone rang. She gave me a glare as if to warn me not to sneak off and then walked over to a far corner to take the call. I strained my ears to hear who answered, but a commotion arose from the lobby, and then Mart came floating in, accompanied by the other ghosts. I'd begun to wonder where he'd gone.

"They can't arrest you," he said indignantly. "We'll get rid of her. Want me to pour a bucket of ice on her head?"

"Not a good idea, Mart," I murmured, hoping she was too focused on the phone call to pay full attention to her surroundings.

"I don't see why not," said Jonathan from behind him. "She needs to cool down, if you ask me."

He wasn't wrong, but we'd antagonised her enough already, and setting a group of aggravated ghosts on her would only prove her point.

Allie cleared her throat. "Maura, who were those… those ogres?"

"The Wardens," I answered. "Is there a local branch in the region?"

"Nope," Jia answered. "Hawkwood Hollow is outside of any local authority, as I found out when I left town. Same reason nobody noticed the lack of a Reaper."

"Then she must have gone farther afield to find them," I concluded. "I wish I knew who told her a demon caused her husband's death."

Not Harold, of course. The Reaper had come to my defence unexpectedly when Shelton had come nosing around town, but would he be able to do the same to the Wardens? Yes, he'd been neglecting his own duties for the past two decades and surely didn't want to talk to the Reaper Council himself either, but he certainly wouldn't defend our ghost-tour business. He'd already implied that Jonas's death was partly our fault.

As for finding the demon? I had little chance of pulling that off without the Wardens' help, since I hadn't the faintest clue *where* the demon was currently hiding. Did Esther? If she did, she wouldn't share it with me, so I grabbed my phone instead. Parker's blog was still open, and while whoever had resurrected his review of our inn ought to be the least of my concerns, the demon had killed him too.

"What're you looking up?" Jia peered at my phone. "Parker's blog. You think there might be something in there?"

"I'm out of any other ideas." I began scrolling through his posts. "If we can find out who's in his account, then it might help us figure out who told her about the demon. Or we can find out why it targeted him, perhaps."

She glanced at Esther, correctly guessing who I meant by 'her.' "Worth a shot."

"Exactly." I kept one eye on Esther as I skimmed through Parker's blog, looking for clues that pointed to how he'd ended up with a demon on his tail.

I soon discovered that his acerbic tone was consistent across all his reviews, and that nobody seemed worthy of praise from him. I rolled my eyes at a particularly eloquent paragraph in which he proclaimed that there were only two people who were deserving of his elusive five-star rating and one of those was himself. "I wonder who the second is?"

"Hmm?" Jia scrolled down her own phone screen. "Hey… Maura. Does this look familiar to you?"

I peered over her shoulder and saw a photo of what appeared to be the country lane leading out of Hawkwood Hollow under one of Parker's blog posts.

"When was this?" I squinted, seeing someone else standing just out of the frame. "Wait… is that Sofia?"

Jia tilted her head, examining the feminine figure standing at the left side of the photo. "You know… I think it is. They knew one another?"

"That would explain a lot." I lifted my head. "I bet she's the second person he's willing to give five stars to—and I'd bet you anything she's the one operating his blog from beyond the grave."

"Who?" Allie asked. "What are you two doing?"

"I think Sofia Granger is Parker's accomplice," I whispered to her. "I know she already checked out of the inn, but did she leave any way to contact her?"

"I have her number." Her gaze flickered to Esther. "If it helps you, I'll fetch it for you."

As she hurried across to the lobby, the ghosts hovered

anxiously in the background, unseen by anyone but me and Jia. Esther's jaw twitched when Allie walked out of sight, but she didn't move to intercept her, though she did grip the phone tighter.

After several tense moments, Allie returned with the bookings list for our ghost tours and showed me the right number and email address for me to contact Sofia. I inputted the number into my phone, and a beep followed.

This number does not exist.

"Oh no." I was willing to bet her email address was the same. "I think she gave fake contact information... do you have Parker's number?"

"You think she might have his phone?" Jia guessed. "I suppose it's worth a try."

She motioned to Allie to hand over the list, her phone in her other hand. I frowned in confusion and then saw Esther had finished her own call and was eyeing the three of us as if she'd caught us raiding her cellar.

"What on earth are you doing?" Esther marched across the room, her lips compressed into a thin line of anger. "Calling backup? I don't think so."

She pulled out her wand, which I stared at for one confused moment. I'd forgotten she might carry one, since her tongue was enough of a weapon on its own. *Ack.*

"Not backup." My hand twitched towards the pocket where I kept my own wand. "Are you acquainted with Sofia Granger?"

She blinked. "What business is it of yours?"

She'd recognised the name. That was enough proof for me. "She's an ex-coven member, and—"

Esther lifted her wand, which went off with a loud bang. All three of us dove behind the bar to avoid being hit, and the sound of glass shattering rang through the air. *Whoa.* She'd officially lost her mind, right when we might finally have nailed down the real culprit.

Jia crouched beside me, her phone's screen flashing with Parker's number. "I've got through to someone…"

An indistinct voice sounded on the other end, drowned out by the sound of another of Esther's spells. Hoping the police would show up soon, I pulled out my own wand.

"Hey!" Jia shouted down the phone. "Dammit—she hung up, but I'm sure it was Sofia whose voice I heard. She has Parker's phone."

"And she knows we're on to her." We had to track her down—after we stopped Esther's rampage. I ducked out from behind the bar and sent a freeze-frame spell at Esther, which missed and knocked down one of our ghost-tour posters. I was lucky it hadn't been worse, and if we weren't careful, she'd completely trash the place.

"Mart," I said out of the corner of my mouth, "now is an excellent time to drop some ice on her head."

"Way ahead of you." A bucket of ice floated past our hiding place, while Allie crouched down behind me.

"Maura—you should go," she whispered. "You're her target, and I don't think those Wardens would mind you leaving the inn if they knew she was attacking you."

"I'm not running away." If Drew was having trouble convincing his fellow officers to help, they might change their minds if they knew we were under attack. "I'll fetch Drew. You two stay hidden, and the ghosts will help you hold her off. Don't put yourself in harm's way."

Darkness spread beneath my feet, and I leapt into the shadows. When I emerged in front of the police station, Drew startled at the sight of me. So did his fellow officers, who jumped and exclaimed in alarm. Oops. I hadn't meant to materialise in front of the entire police force, but I'd assumed they were still inside the police station. Nothing for it. I looked directly at Drew. "Esther has lost her mind and is firing spells at the inn. We need backup before someone gets hurt."

"You'll have to wait," said Petra, my least favourite of Drew's officers. "There's been a jailbreak, and that's our priority."

"No," Drew said. "We can help with both. I'll go—"

"A breakout?" My blood turned to ice. "Did the ex-coven members escape jail?"

"Yes—how did you know?" Petra's eyes narrowed in suspicion. "This seems coordinated, and someone wanted us distracted."

"I think it was Sofia." I turned back to Drew. "We found out that Sofia Granger and Parker Maven knew one another, and she has access to all his online accounts. She answered when Jia called Parker's phone too."

Drew swore. "You think she's the summoner?"

"Yes, and the Wardens are after the wrong person." I had to tell them their client had gone rogue and started attacking us, too, so I hoped Harold had already done a decent enough job defending my good name that they wouldn't react to my appearance by slapping a pair of hand-cuffs on me. "I'll be right back. You—go and help Allie at the inn."

I ran up the road to the cemetery gate, where the two Wardens stood outside the Reaper's cottage. Upon seeing my approach, one ogre swivelled on the spot and bared his tusks at me. "I thought I told you not to leave the inn."

"Esther has her wand out and is trying to curse us," I said. "Also, several criminals just broke out of our local prison, and I think the person who helped them escape was also the one who summoned the demon. We have to—"

"We?" growled the ogre. "No, you'll come back to our office to explain yourself thoroughly before we do anything."

"Esther is trying to curse my boss and coworkers. I can't leave."

"How exactly did you get here so fast?" asked the second ogre. "I thought you didn't use your Reaper abilities at all."

Uh-oh. "I ran. Look, did you not hear me say that a group of coordinated criminals just escaped jail with the help of the demon's summoner?"

"The head of your police department was adamant that he didn't need the help of any outsiders, was he not?" growled the first ogre. "As for Esther, we will walk back to the inn to talk to her, but you won't be allowed to run this time."

As one of them pulled out a pair of handcuffs, I backed up a step. "The person who summoned the demon is getting away as we speak. If you put me in handcuffs, I can't find her."

"You expect us to believe you after the way you've behaved already?"

Well, no. But I could see how this scenario would play out. They'd drag me to their bosses and put me through hours-long interrogations while the jailed witches got back to Mina Devlin, the demon remained at large, and the real killer got away with their crimes.

Screw it. As the ogres grabbed for me, I twisted away and vanished into the shadows.

14

No doubt I'd regret my decision later, but the relief at escaping the ogres' clutches flooded my body with adrenaline. As I landed in the inn's entryway, the first thing I saw were the ghosts, who scattered in alarm when I materialised among them.

The second thing I saw was Esther... or rather, a statue that looked like her. Her body was frozen stiff, as if someone had coated her in ice from head to toe.

I blinked in confusion. "Who did that?"

"Brian, mostly," Mart answered, holding up the empty ice bucket proudly. "I helped."

"Nice one." I strode over to Allie and Jia, who were in the process of cleaning up the mess of upended tables and chairs that Esther's misfired spells had knocked askew. "Hey. I can't stay long, since I may be on the run from the authorities."

Jia lifted her head. "Seriously? Wait, you don't mean the police?"

"No, they're preoccupied because a bunch of people broke out of jail," I said. "To be precise, Mina Devlin's allies are once again at large."

She cursed and sprang to her feet. "*Sofia.* I've been trying to get through to her via Parker's phone, but without any luck. I bet she's on the run."

"Or on her way to meet the escapees," I guessed. "The Wardens refused to help. They took Drew's command to stay out of our town's business to heart and said the police would have to recapture them."

"Great." She swivelled to the frozen form of Esther. "I don't know how long she'll stay like that, but if I had to guess, Sofia sent her as a distraction."

"Was Esther herself aware of that?"

"I have no idea," she said. "Why are you on the run, then?"

"I used my Reaper abilities to escape the Wardens when they tried to handcuff me," I admitted, which elicited a groan from Allie. "I had to make sure you were okay, and besides, someone has to stop Sofia. Not to mention the demon she summoned. If the Wardens dragged me into an interrogation, then it would be too late."

Jia's brow wrinkled. "We don't know where Sofia is."

"Littlewood," I said with certainty. "She and Parker were friends, so they must have lived near to one another. It's a starting point, anyway."

"Then I'll go with you," Jia offered. "You need backup."

I shook my head. "Not if that demon is still running around. It can't kill Reapers, but anyone else is fair game."

"And what if Mina and her allies are waiting for you?" she asked. "Trust me, I'm more than ready to take on the coven, even Mina Devlin herself, if I have to."

From the determined set to her jaw and the knowledge that she'd waited for this moment for a long time, I knew I wouldn't be able to convince her otherwise. "All right, but I need to take out that demon first. Drew's team is prepared to recapture the escapees, but they won't be able to see the demon until it's too late."

Even the Wardens wouldn't, and who knew, maybe saving their ungrateful hides would be enough for them not to arrest me when this was over. I could dream.

"I'll hold the fort here," Allie told us. "Also, if the Wardens come back here, I'll tell them I didn't see you, Maura."

"Good call." I beckoned to Mart. "Want to come? Or would you rather stay behind?"

"All aboard the Reaper Express," he said in answer.

Jia wore a slightly wary expression when she approached the shadows swirling around my feet—travelling by Reaper was not a fun experience for the average person—and placed her hand on my arm.

The three of us vanished into the shadows, emerging on a deserted country lane that led from Hawkwood Hollow to its neighbours. Since I'd never been to Littlewood before, this was as far as I could bring us without having to walk. Part of me expected to see the escaped prisoners lurking in a nearby field, but there didn't appear to be anyone around, including Sofia.

Jia took in a shaky breath and pointed northward. "Littlewood is that way. The police won't have got there yet."

"I know." Even the Wardens would take a while to catch up on foot, which played in our favour, considering I was as much a target as the escaped witches were. "We need to find Sofia, but I don't know that calling Parker's number will point us to her location."

"No, but I have his address," Jia said. "I found it while you were gone. Sofia probably won't be in his house, but his housemates might know where she lives."

"Good thinking."

Mart drifted behind as the two of us walked the short distance to Littlewood. Jia used her phone to navigate the way through the narrow, cobbled streets until we came to a road lined with terraced houses. Student houses, judging by the loud music that drifted from an open window and the large quantity of empty beer cans filling the recycling bins.

Jia knocked on the door to Parker's house, and a gangly wizard with long ropy dark hair answered, a pair of red earbuds in his ears. "Who are you?"

I cleared my throat. "You don't know me, but I was an, ah, acquaintance of Parker Maven."

"You're the second person who's come here claiming that." He eyed Jia, then me, his gaze passing right over Mart. "I've never seen either of you before."

Suspicion gripped me. "Was the second person who came here an elderly woman, by any chance?"

"I'm guessing yes," Jia added. "We're not here for the same reasons as her, but we'd appreciate it if you told us if you've seen Sofia Granger. She and Parker were friends."

"Sofia?" One of his earbuds fell out. "Yeah, we've met. She used to come and visit."

Gotcha. "We need to find her, but I don't know her address."

"Neither do I." He put the earbud back in. "I don't want any part in this. Leave me alone."

The door closed in our faces, and I took a step back. "What was that for?"

"Sofia might have warned him not to answer the door to strangers." Jia paced away from the house. "Or Esther scared him earlier. What should we do now? Start knocking on doors and hope that we find Sofia?"

"Excuse me?" Mart pointedly poked a finger through the wall. "Have you forgotten you have a ghost with you? In fact, *you* can walk through walls if you like, Maura."

"Only if I don't mind being accused of breaking and entering on top of running from the law." I spoke in a low voice in case Parker's housemate could hear us. "You should be fine, though."

"Oh, no." He threw up his hands. "I'm not doing more free labour for you. Forget it."

"You're the one who made the suggestion." I glimpsed Parker's housemate peering through the curtains and glared at him until he disappeared. "Please, Mart. You know what'll happen to you if the Reaper Council shows up before we stop Sofia."

He pouted. "Fine, fine."

My brother floated directly through the wall of the nearest house, vanishing through the bricks. It wasn't the most efficient way to search the village for a single person, but it wouldn't cause as much of a stir as me using my Reaper powers to do the same.

Jia and I found a spot to wait which was out of sight of any windows while Mart continued his search, zipping in and out of each house and making spooky noises. At least one of us was enjoying themselves.

Several tense minutes passed before Mart came whizzing back to our sides. "I found a ghost-proofed house. I bet that's hers."

"Of course she ghost-proofed the place." The spell I'd found in Esther's room at the inn had been her work, too, I was sure. "Let's move."

Jia and I followed Mart through a warren of tight streets until we came to another small, unremarkable brick house. I couldn't even see the ghost-proof defences that had kept Mart out, but I approached the door warily all the same. If Sofia was allied with the coven, she was bound to be prepared to deal with a Reaper.

"I'll go in first," I told Jia. "If that demon is in there, I don't want you taken unawares."

She opened her mouth to argue then shook her head. "All right, but I'll be ready if she tries to run."

"I bet she will." I stepped into shadows, envisioning the sliver of room I could see through a gap in the curtains.

When I emerged into a living room, Sofia lurched away from me with a screech of alarm. Her reaction was a far cry from her smug attitude when we'd last encountered her, though in fairness, I'd have jumped out of my skin if a Reaper had leapt out of the wall at me, and I *was* one.

Sofia ran for the nearest door, but I'd been prepared. Marshalling the extent of my Reaper influence over the afterworld, I willed the darkness to fill the space around us and flood the room. She could theoretically walk straight through the shadow if she liked, but the sight of her escape route blanketed in shadow stopped her in her tracks.

"Didn't think I'd track you down here, did you?" I couldn't quell a hint of triumph from entering my tone. "What the hell are you playing at?"

"I don't know what you mean," she squeaked. "You're breaking the law."

"*You* helped with a jailbreak, so I don't think you're in any position to lecture me about rule-breaking."

She shook her head frantically. "What are you talking about?"

"Don't deny it," Jia said from the other side of the front door. "You're the one who's meddling with Parker's blog, aren't you? Did he know you planned to have him killed?"

"No!" she insisted. "Of course I didn't. We were friends."

"Then why do you have his phone?" I queried. "In fact, why are you so determined to shut us down?"

She shook her head. "Your business *should* be shut down. You're a rogue Reaper."

"You don't know the first thing about the Reapers," I said. "I suppose you've been goading Esther into coming after us too. Does *she* know who really killed her husband?"

"I don't know what you mean," she repeated, her voice increasingly high-pitched. "You're breaking and entering."

"Trust me, it's better for all of us if you're honest with me," I said. "That demon—did you summon it? Or did someone else?"

She shook her head in answer, eyeing the shadows around me as if looking for an escape route. I wasn't about to let her realise she wasn't trapped at all, so I stepped closer to her and forced her to back further against the wall to avoid me. "Sofia, I'm inclined to believe that you didn't intend for Parker to die, but if you tell me where that demon is hiding, then I can deal with it before anyone else is hurt. Including you."

Sofia edged along the wall. "Why do you care?"

"Because I want to get rid of it." Whether she'd been the original summoner or not, it couldn't be more obvious she was in over her head. I might not know *why* she'd summoned a demon, but she hadn't intended it to escape, and I assumed that she and her allies had tried to deflect blame from themselves for Jonas's death by manipulating his widow into joining in with their crusade against the inn. In the process, they'd left her oblivious to the fact that they were the killers and not us.

When Sofia didn't reply, I went on, "The coven is behind this, aren't they? You joined up with Mina Devlin again after she left Hawkwood Hollow."

She glared at me. "I don't need to hear any judgement from someone who has no coven and never will."

"That wasn't as much of a put-down as you think, trust me." I glared straight back at her. "If you're allied with Mina Devlin, you're better off without a coven at all."

"You have no idea what you've done by throwing her out of town, Maura," she said. "If anything else happens, it's on you."

"What's that supposed to mean?"

She closed her eyes for a moment as if to steady her nerves. Then she whispered an inaudible word, and the shadows *moved*.

My gaze fell on a circle of herbs scattered on the carpet by her feet, near-hidden by the shadows. *The demon. She called it here.*

Darkness returned—not of my own making, but a swirling pillar that resolved itself into a form vaguely shaped like a person. I stood firm despite the chills reaching deep into my bones, knowing it couldn't hurt me—but there was another living target in the room.

The demon might have no face, but I sensed it change direction all the same, and Sofia yelped and ran for the door. Not fast enough. As she grabbed the door and yanked it open, the darkness swarmed over her back like a fast-acting rash.

A startled Jia watched from the doorway as Sofia fell forwards, her body crumpling to the floor.

"Hey!" I twisted on the spot, my gaze seeking out the shadowy figure, but it had already vanished through the open door. I ran to Jia's side and grabbed her arm, dragging her over the threshold. "Don't move."

"What?" She eyed Sofia's body in bafflement. "Is she dead?"

"Yeah, she summoned the demon into her house." And then she'd opened the front door and let it escape into the surrounding neighbourhood. I wasn't about to risk Jia's safety by summoning it back in here, but Sofia had put everyone in the region in danger. "She didn't know it couldn't hurt me."

"What was she thinking would happen?" Mart floated to Jia's side. "Did she think she'd be spared?"

"Quite possibly, yes."

I stepped around her body, nudging her outstretched arm back over the doorstep. We didn't need the neighbours to spot her, but someone would come looking for her eventually, and if we stayed here, the odds of us taking the blame were depressingly high.

I closed the door to the house. "I need to find that demon, but it's loose in a residential area. I know it can only attack one person at a time, but it can move as fast as a ghost." Or a Reaper.

"Yeah." Jia cursed under her breath. "Where do you want to go? Back to Hawkwood Hollow?"

"No—I want to find the police first." I beckoned her to my side. "That okay with you?"

She drew in a breath. "All right."

I might have taken us to Drew's side, but he might still be dealing with Esther, and there was a chance the other police officers had joined with the Wardens. I didn't need to end up in cuffs, so I opted to take us to the country road outside the village instead.

The three of us vanished through the shadows once more. When we landed, Jia staggered away from me and swore. "Dammit. We have company."

We did—and not the police. A group of witches approached the village, and I recognised Marie and Angela among them. Mina Devlin's allies. *Ah hell.*

15

I'd miscalculated. The police were nowhere to be seen, but Mina Devlin's cronies blocked our path. I recognised Angela and Marie among them, but the woman herself was conspicuously absent. *Where's she hiding?*

"You." Recovering first, Angela reached for her wand. "I expected you to stick your nose in sooner, Reaper, but I suppose you're a little slow."

"This is not going to end the way you think it is." My hand twitched towards my own wand, but magic wouldn't be enough to subdue a half-dozen witches at the same time. To do that, I'd need to use my Reaper powers, but I wanted answers first. "Where's your boss?"

"Oh, don't worry, she's waiting for you," said Marie. "She's been itching to make you pay for your crimes."

"Or hiding," Jia added. "You do know your demon just killed one of your own allies, don't you? Sofia's dead."

Marie barely blinked. "She knew the risks when she signed up."

That figured. The question was, where the hell were the police? I assumed it'd been Sofia who'd let the prisoners out, but one thing was clear—she and her allies had wanted Drew to be distracted, and they'd gone as far as to convince Esther to drag the Wardens to Hawkwood Hollow in order to ensure nobody would stand in their way.

"Delightful," Jia said. "I'd have thought you'd know the risks of setting a beast from the afterworld loose with no plan to recapture it if it ends up turning on you."

I would have thought so, too, but they'd also hampered my chances of finding allies without risking them becoming targets for the demon.

"That was a risk we were willing to take," Angela said.

"To achieve what?" I queried. "I assume my allies were supposed to be the original targets, but Reapers are immune to being hurt by demons, as Mina Devlin ought to know."

No, I hadn't been the target, not if she wanted to deal with me herself.

"To persuade you to leave the safety of Hawkwood Hollow, of course." Angela advanced on the pair of us, wand in hand. "I assumed you wouldn't be able to resist trying to track the demon down."

"Not when you were trying to frame me for murder." If I'd shown up at Parker's house after his death as they'd evidently expected, I'd have run the risk of taking the blame if the invisible assailant had been long gone. "Three people are dead thanks to you."

Not that I should have expected anything less of Mina Devlin's allies. They were unscrupulous. I drew my wand, reaching for my Reaper abilities as I did so, and darkness pooled around my feet.

"Stop her!" Marie jabbed a finger in my direction, and jets of light shot from her allies' wands.

Jia and I ducked, but there was nowhere to run. Jia's wand flew from her grip as she toppled onto her back, her body frozen stiff. *Dammit.* I grabbed her arm, intending to drag her through the shadows to safety, but another spell knocked my own wand spiralling from my grip.

The shadows receded at once, and Marie let out a triumphant cry. "That's it. You can't use your shadows to escape now, Reaper."

No. They'd cut off my Reaper powers *and* disarmed me in the same instant. Angela's mouth curved in a satisfied smile as she pointed her wand at me—

The sudden blare of an alarm went off, startling all the witches. I leapt for my wand and seized it, but by the time I was on my feet, Marie had grabbed Jia's arm.

"No!"

The group of witches waved their wands in unison, and they all vanished—taking Jia with them.

The sound of the alarm, which sounded like it belonged to a car, continued to echo down the country lane. I looked for the source, and Mart came over to my side. "Didn't know what else to do."

"They took Jia." I scanned the road and retrieved her wand from where she'd dropped it. "I don't know where they went."

I couldn't follow them even if I did, because my Reaper abilities were shut off. If I had to guess, they'd used the same spell they'd tested out when I'd unwittingly put my hand on a booby trap the conspirators had set up at the witches' headquarters. Jia had removed it with a general hex-removal spell, but with her gone, nobody would be able to take the spell off me unless I found another witch. I'd have to return to Hawkwood Hollow and hope that Jia could hold out until I was able to come to help. I could only hope they kept her alive as bait, because she didn't have a Reaper's immunity to death by demon and was entirely at their mercy. Mina Devlin wouldn't make the same mistake that Sofia had.

"Maura." Mart waved a transparent hand in front of my face. "Standing here isn't going to help her."

I swore under my breath. "I have to get rid of the demon first."

I hated the very notion of leaving Jia to her fate, but they'd taken her as a hostage for a purpose, and even the act of following her might endanger her life. If I took out their demon, I eliminated any chance of them using it on my allies, including her.

"Are you sure?" Mart asked.

"I'm sure." I broke into a fast stride in the direction of Hawkwood Hollow and then halted for a second time when I spied another group of people marching purposefully down the country road. "Who're they?"

"The police." Mart flew ahead of me. "Drew's with them."

"Oh, good." I began to jog towards them until Drew spotted me. Holding up a hand to warn his fellow officers not to attack, he came to meet me. "Maura, what're you doing out here?"

"Drew—they cut off my Reaper powers and took Jia." I raised my voice to the officers behind him. "Who has a wand? I need someone to take this spell off me if I want to find them."

"Who is 'them'?" asked another officer.

"I imagine she's referring to our escaped prisoners," said Drew. "It sounds as if they've taken a hostage too."

"Yeah—and they said Mina Devlin is calling the shots." I spoke fast. "I don't know where their hideout is, but I assume it's in the area. Can someone take the spell off me so I can find them? A simple hex-removal charm will do the trick."

Drew addressed his officers. "Any volunteers? Maura's telling the truth. If anyone can remove the spell, it'll help us find our criminals."

Gratitude washed over me. Drew was on my side, but I

couldn't risk him and his fellow officers being targeted by the demon, either.

A wizard hesitantly stepped forwards, but another officer held out an arm to stop him. Petra. A jolt of irritation hit me. "We don't all trust your word, Maura," she said. "I heard you're on the run from the Wardens."

Ack. "We had a misunderstanding. Look, that demon has already killed three people, including one of the witches' own allies, and any of you might be next. If I want to avoid losing anyone else, then I'll have to get rid of the demon."

"Then you plan to run off, don't you?" said Petra.

"No, I'm not running." I levelled her with a glare. "Whatever your personal problem is with me, I doubt you know the first thing about summoning and banishing demonic spirits that can kill someone with a touch. I *can* get rid of the demon, but not with my Reaper powers switched off."

"Go on." Drew beckoned to the wizard to step forwards. "Maura is the witches' target, no doubt, so they'll want her to be able to find their hideout. We can wait for her to get rid of that creature first."

The wizard flicked his wand, and relief arose when I called the shadows and they returned to my hands—at least until a different shadow entirely stirred in the corner of my vision. This one, shaped like a person, moved swiftly towards the officers.

"The demon!" I pointed, frantic, but of course most of them couldn't see the shadowy attacker. "Hey—leave them alone!"

I ran straight at the demon and called my own shadows, darkness cloaking my steps as I tackled it head-on. Tackling a demon brought a sensation best compared to that of running through an ice-cold waterfall, but my grip snagged on a solidity beneath the shadows, an essence that only a Reaper would be able to feel.

This would be easier with a scythe, I thought, not for the first time, as I grabbed a handful of nebulous shadow. Nearby, the officers had scattered in a panic, spooked by the sight of me seemingly wrestling with thin air on a carpet of shadows.

The figure squirmed out of my grip, but I followed, and the pair of us toppled into the darkness. A familiar sight met us on the other side: Hawkwood Hollow's main high street. Why had it come here?

Shadows flooded my palms again, but the dark figure had already escaped my grasp. Worse, several people were out on the street, gaping at my sudden appearance. Nobody else was able to resist the demon aside from me... with one other exception.

I stepped into the shadows again and pictured the Reaper's cottage. His loud cursing greeted me as I stumbled out of the dark, my feet catching on a pile of junk in the middle of his living room.

"You!" he bellowed, lurching to his feet from an armchair. "Get out of my house."

"Sorry," I said. "You're the only person aside from me that the demon won't kill on sight. It's here—it's here in Hawkwood Hollow."

"Get out!"

"Can I borrow your scythe?"

I didn't wait for an answer. As I ran to grab the scythe from where he'd leaned it against a wall, he stalked over to me, his mouth set in an angry line. "I've had enough of you. I already sent away those Wardens on your behalf, but I can't stop them from arresting you when they come back. You'll have to leave."

Leave. Meaning leave Hawkwood Hollow itself. If not for my ongoing fear for the others, I'd have felt the impact of that word harder, but I couldn't afford to think on what that meant. Not now.

"Look, this is Mina Devlin's work, not mine," I said. "She summoned the demon—or one of her allies did, and they paid the price for it. Now the demon's here, and until it's gone, nobody is safe."

"Except for me," he said sourly. "I'm honoured."

"Trust me, this isn't ideal." It also wasn't fair. I should have had the chance to say goodbye to the others at the very least. Allie and Carey deserved much better, but I was doing this for them—and Jia too.

My hand closed around the scythe's end, but Harold didn't stop me from taking it. Nor did he react when I stepped into the shadows and reappeared in a deserted street by the river.

"Demon, come here," I called to the darkness. "I command you to answer me."

My voice echoed, infused with a commanding tone that no spirit could resist. I raised the scythe and my voice in tandem. "Demon. Come."

The beast appeared in my field of vision, reluctant but unable to resist answering the call of a Reaper. I'd crossed a line, make no mistake, but going full Reaper had its perks. The demon moved closer until I brought the scythe down in an arc, parting the darkness like the folds of a curtain.

The demon vanished, its shadowy form sucked into the ether. I exhaled in a long breath, lowering the scythe. My heart hammered, the Reaper in me satisfied at a job well done even as the human part of me recoiled from the sheer inhumanity of the instrument in my hand.

I should have used the shadows to shortcut back to the Reaper's cottage, but I walked on shaky feet instead, as if to remind myself I was still a solid being myself. Still human.

When I spotted two surly-looking ogres out of the corner of my eye, I snapped out of my stupor. Oh hell. They'd stayed, and if I went back to the Reaper's cottage, they'd seize me at once.

Jia. I needed to save her from Mina and her allies, and that meant embracing the shadows again.

I pictured her face, imagined following a thread connecting me to Jia. *Find her,* I thought, and darkness came back like an old friend.

I landed in a small room, swathed in darkness almost as thick as the afterworld. A flickering bulb hung from the ceiling, showing me that Mina Devlin wasn't here, but Jia lay on the floor, alone. She lifted her head groggily. "Maura?"

"Sorry I left you." I pointed my wand at her and cast a spell that undid the ropes securing her wrists and ankles. "Are you okay?"

The witches must have taken off the immobilising spell, but she still looked a little dazed, and when I handed over her wand, she didn't move.

"You have a scythe," she said. "I'm not imagining that, am I?"

"Nope. Is this Mina's safe house?"

"I haven't seen her, but I've only seen this room." She grimaced and rubbed the back of her head. "I think they threw me in here and then ran off."

"Drew's team is on their way, but I overtook them." I helped her to her feet with my free hand, holding the scythe in the other. Using it against Mina and her allies would be a massive violation of the Reapers' rules and make my previous transgressions look tame. A Reaper who used their tools to take the lives of the living would face instant execution, and besides, it wasn't a fate I wanted to inflict on anyone, even Mina's allies. The scythe would be effective enough as a scare tactic, though I theoretically shouldn't need to worry about breaking any more rules when I was already doomed. The Wardens had seen me use my Reaper powers, and while Drew had the authority to get rid of them, that wouldn't stop them from coming back —and bringing the Reaper Council with them next time. The quicker I ran from Hawkwood Hollow, the better, but not before Mina and her allies answered for their crimes.

After checking Jia was capable of standing on her own, I cast an unlocking charm on the door. When I stepped out into the corridor, two witches came running into view. Both stopped dead—excuse the pun—when they saw the instrument in my hands.

"Hey, there." I bared my teeth and lifted the scythe. "Does Mina still want to talk to me?"

The colour drained from their faces. It was mildly satisfying to watch, if nothing else, though I didn't actually have a plan as to what to do next. When more witches came running down the stairs and out of the nearby rooms, I lifted the sceptre higher, projecting my voice. "*Does* Mina want to talk to me?"

Nobody answered. Jia waved her wand, disarming one of the witches, but the corridor was narrow, and there were too many of them to fight off using regular magic. I had to take these witches down before they realised that I had no intention of using the scythe on them.

Two of the witches vanished in a flash of light, a transportation spell, while Jia continued to fire spells at the rest. A couple of them had dropped their wands, and they flinched away when I advanced on them.

"Take me to your boss or I'll cut you down," I bluffed. "Go on."

"She's not here," Marie squeaked. "This is a safe house."

"I don't think you're being honest." Maybe she was, though. She'd wanted to lure me into a trap but had taken a risk in making it relatively easy for me to find their location.

If we were close to Littlewood, then the police weren't far off either.

The sound of a door crashing open made me glance behind me. Jia had managed to kick the front door open, and a familiar country lane lay on the other side. I'd guessed right, and we really weren't far from the village at all.

Marie grabbed her wand and scrambled upright, gearing up to flee too. *No you don't.*

Zipping through the shadows to their side, I gave the remaining witches my most terrifying Reaper stare. "Take me to Mina."

"No!" Marie shrank away from my scythe. "I won't tell you a thing."

"Then maybe you'll tell *them*." Jia gestured to the doorway, through which several police officers were visible on the driveway leading up the house. Including—

Drew. His eyes flew wide at the sight of the scythe in my hand, but as his fellow officers approached the house, he swiftly recovered. "Police here. Nobody move!"

Between a Reaper and arrest, the choice was obvious, and with Jia's encouragement, the witches came hurrying out of the house. The scythe was more of a hindrance to me than anything, since I didn't want to accidentally hit anyone with it, friendly or otherwise. Instead, I stood and watched as the police brought the dazed witches out of the house and lined them up on the drive.

I ought to leave before the Wardens showed up, but the notion of leaving Drew—for good, potentially—tore my heart in two. As I racked my mind for a way out, Mart came drifting over to me, looking peeved. "Thanks for leaving me behind."

The answer clicked into place. "You brought the police here."

"Obviously."

Some of the officers must be able to see ghosts, then, but it was a miracle he'd convinced them to follow his directions at all.

"Sorry I left you," I said. "It was kind of an emergency."

"Nice scythe."

I grunted. "Harold will want it back."

And then… then I'd have to face my future, however bleak it might look. Yet I stayed, watching, while Drew's officers took the prisoners away.

"Ready to go home?" he asked, not knowing how much those words hurt to hear.

"Yes," answered Jia, who'd stalled in the act of following the officers and their prisoners. "Right, Maura?"

"You need to go to the hospital." I swallowed a lump in my throat. "Drew, I have to return the scythe to its owner. Then… then I'm not staying."

Confusion filtered through his expression, horror swift on its heels. "What—you think the Reaper Council will come after you?"

"The Wardens saw me use my Reaper powers, Drew," I said quietly. "There's nothing I can say to convince them otherwise."

He swore under his breath. Then he embraced me and placed a kiss on my lips. "I *will* come back for you, Maura. I promise."

I nodded, blinking hard. "Mart?"

"I'm with you."

"So am I," said Jia, as I took her arm. "Don't run, Maura. Please."

"I have to." I closed my eyes, and darkness arose to embrace us.

16

___

Cathy nearly jumped out of her skin when we landed in her room at the hospital, and I didn't really blame her for pointing her wand at me.

"Jia needs help," I said, without preamble. "Mina's allies hit her with a spell, and I want someone to check her over."

"Hey!" Jia herself said indignantly. "You can't leave me behind."

"Did you say *Mina*?" Then Cathy did a double take. "What... why do you have a scythe?"

"Borrowed it," I said. "I can't stick around, but I wanted to make sure Jia got to a healer before I leave."

"She's not leaving," Jia said. "And *I'm* not staying. What're you brewing in that cauldron? It smells like a pair of old socks."

Cathy blinked at us. "Look, you can't disappear without telling me what's going on. If Mina's in town, then do the police need my help—?"

"They already recaptured the prisoners," I told her. "Mina isn't here, don't worry."

Jia's shout of indignation followed me into the darkness

as I pictured the Reaper's cottage in my mind's eye. This time I landed in front of a furious Harold… and the two Wardens, who flanked him. I dropped the scythe with a curse.

"Ah—I'm just returning the Reaper's property," I told the Wardens. "I know I broke the rules, but don't punish Allie and Carey, or Drew, or Jia, or anyone who covered for me."

As I made to escape into the afterworld, old Harold *moved*, grabbing my arm. I reeled, the shadows abruptly receding from my reach.

"Hey!" I protested. "I thought you were on my side. You know what happens to me if the Reaper Council comes here. Not just me."

Every ghost in town would be in danger. My friends would be, too, for helping me, and the inn… surely he understood that it wasn't for my own sake that I was leaving.

"There are exceptions to the rules," said Harold. "Even with the Reaper Council. Now will you sit down?"

He *wanted* me to stay inside his cottage? The Wardens didn't move to grab me either, though they might be reluctant to get near the shadows curling around the Reaper's hands. In any case, I didn't have much choice but to sink into a seat. The past few hours had worn me out, and without the scythe in my hands any longer, the trembling in my limbs made itself known.

I couldn't keep running. That much was obvious. But I didn't have safe houses set up like Mina evidently did. All I had was the truth. I didn't even have my brother. Mart must have stayed outside, or at the hospital, and I didn't blame him a bit.

Harold jerked his head at the Wardens. "Tell her everything so she stops trying to run."

"Your fellow Reaper explained the situation," growled one of the ogres. "It's my understanding that you banished the rogue demon using your Reaper abilities."

"Yes, I know I broke the rules," I said wearily. "You tend to make exceptions when the people you care about are in danger, and that demon already killed three people. The witches sent it after me, but Reapers are immune, so it would have targeted anyone who went near me if I hadn't sent it into the deeper afterworld."

"Yes, I gathered," growled the Warden. "You acted rashly, but there's a clause in the Reaper rules for life-or-death situations."

There was? If so, that didn't erase the fact that I'd used my Reaper skills in other situations, not life-threatening ones. Or that I'd resisted arrest and run away.

"Also," said the other Warden, "the Reaper Council is in charge of these decisions. Or rather, the head Reaper of your region."

My mouth went dry. "I know, but look—if you send me to the town where I grew up, then they'll come here afterwards."

"The local Reaper representative is already here," said the ogre.

"He means me," said Harold. "Enough dancing around the subject. Shelton and I came to an understanding that I'm the person to be consulted in situations like this, as the lead Reaper in this town, and I've explained that to the Wardens too."

"You?" I hadn't intended to sound quite as incredulous as I did, but it was common knowledge that he'd resigned from his position without any intention of going back to being an active Reaper. If I hadn't already been sitting down, my legs might well have given out from under me in shock.

"Yes, me," he said impatiently. "You don't even have a scythe, which eliminates you from consideration. I'm the authority in your home, and I've made it clear that you had good reason to act outside of the boundaries of the Council's rules."

"My... home." Wait. "I thought I was automatically assigned to my Reaper parent's community."

"You're as dense as a brick," Harold informed me. "Multiple people vouched for your position as a citizen here, and I expect more will come forwards when they're finished securing their escaped criminals."

My mouth fell open. Who? He must mean Allie and Carey... but it couldn't just be them. Not that I was about to ignore the lifeline he'd offered me. "I mean, I *do* live here, but I thought you'd already made up your minds." I addressed the last part to the Wardens.

"We weren't in full knowledge of all the facts," said one of the ogres in a slightly apologetic tone. "Neither was the woman who hired us."

"Wait, where is Esther now?"

"She's waiting for us at a more suitable location."

Good. She wasn't at the inn. Not that anyone would have left her unsupervised after she'd cracked and started trying to hex us, but that still left a lot of unanswered questions.

"So... what happens now?" I asked the Wardens. "I mean, it should be obvious that I didn't summon that thing. The police are in the process of bringing back their escaped prisoners, who were in touch with the person who *did* summon it, so if you want to get the full story, I'm sure Drew would be willing to let you talk to them."

"They're back?" The two ogres exchanged glances, then one beckoned to me. "Then you will come with us."

That figured. I wasn't off the hook yet, though they didn't put me in handcuffs. When I moved to follow them out of the cottage, Harold didn't offer me any words of encouragement, only an unreadable look.

Outside, I found Mart lurking behind the door. When the ogres walked past, he ducked out of sight.

"Relax, they can't see you," I whispered to him. "You heard all that, didn't you?"

"Yes, but I don't trust them."

Neither did I, but the two ogres made no move to handcuff me even when we were alone together. Instead, they waited for me to catch them up at the cemetery gates and made their way to the police station.

Through the transparent front doors, I saw pandemonium reigned inside the office, with staff running in all directions. I had a brief moment of panic before I saw that the witches remained in handcuffs and the chaos was solely a result of the suddenness of their return. Drew stood at the centre of the lobby, trying to calm everyone down—until he saw me at the door.

At his order, the other officers moved away from the doors to let us in. I ended up pushed to the back as the two massive ogres moved over to talk to Drew. He caught my eye a couple of times, wonder and shock in his expression, but it was impossible for me to give him an explanation with his attention already pulled in several directions at once. Mart went to have a look around and returned with the news that Esther was in the holding cells.

"Really?" I followed him around the outskirts of the lobby and towards the door leading to the holding cells. Most of the witches would be returned to the main part of the jail, but a familiar elderly woman sat on a bench inside one of the cells for temporary prisoners.

When she saw me, her eyes bulged. "You!"

"Me," I said. "We found your husband's killer. You're welcome."

Somehow it had surprised me that she was in jail, but she'd committed assault when she'd attacked Allie and the rest of us, so it made sense that the Wardens had called on the remaining officers to take her into custody so they'd have one fewer person to keep an eye on.

"You should be in my place!" Esther screamed, unable to make herself heard by any of the harried officers running up and down the corridor with their newly returned prisoners. "I want justice."

I gave her an echo of my ominous Reaper stare. "Trust me, as a Reaper, I can tell you with certainty that there's no such thing as justice. Have fun in there."

While she'd probably be let off lightly, she wouldn't be a threat to me any longer. I felt kind of sorry for her for the way Sofia and Parker had used her for their own ends, but not enough to plead for her release. Honestly, since the perpetrators of her husband's death were dead, that was as close to justice as she was going to get.

I left her screaming obscenities and returned to the lobby, where I spotted both Allie and Carey outside. While I probably wasn't supposed to leave, the two Wardens were too busy talking to Drew to notice me join the others—where Allie embraced me. I stiffened, surprised, then let out a muffled gasp when Carey grabbed me in a bear hug from behind that crushed my ribs.

"Thank you," I whispered to them, my eyes stinging. "Thanks for telling them this is my home."

"What else would we do?" Allie asked. "It's true."

"Is it okay, then?" asked Carey. "I mean… are you allowed to stay?"

I looked through the police station doors and caught Drew's eye, sending him a reassuring smile. "Yeah. I think I am."

———

The Wardens didn't leave town until the following day, but they spent most of that time working with the police and filling out paperwork and left the inn alone. While part of me remained worried that they'd change their minds, the reality was that I'd broken no laws and they had no business reporting me to the head of the Reaper Council. Unless they wanted to get me arrested for saving their hides.

The result was that Jia and I returned to work the following day as if nothing had ever interrupted us.

"I can't believe Harold became an active Reaper again," Jia remarked as we were cleaning up at the end of our shift. "Never thought I'd see the day."

"I'm not sure he's planning on actually doing any Reaping, though," I said. "I figured that if he's going to accept that I'm living here, he's going to have to be prepared for this kind of thing to happen on a not-infrequent basis."

Until I took down Mina Devlin for good, she'd keep trying to get at me by any means, legal or not.

As for Esther, she'd left town after her brief stint in a cell without any harm done. She hadn't come to apologise, which came as more of a relief than an annoyance. The restaurant was still a bit quiet, but bookings for our next tour were trickling in, and while Mart said I owed him enough favours to last my entire lifetime, the other ghosts had taken to applauding whenever I entered the room. They'd come through for me in a major way too. They didn't want me to leave any more than my living friends did.

It was a weird feeling, being wanted.

Mart came into the restaurant as I was wiping down the tables. "I deleted that review, by the way. Permanently this time."

"Oh, good." I straightened upright. "Did you change the password?"

"Yes. Are you sure you don't want me to delete the rest of his posts?"

"No," I replied. "Come on, Parker's dead. The best we can do is leave him in peace."

"Not all the dead deserve respect," he answered. "Oh look, your boyfriend's here."

"Just in time." I threw down the wet cloth I'd been using to clean up. I ran halfway across the restaurant, where Drew greeted me with a kiss that made Mart pretend to vomit into the sink. Ignoring him, I returned the gesture with equal enthusiasm.

"Sorry I haven't been around," Drew said, when we finally broke apart. "Those Wardens do like their paperwork."

"What are they actually doing here?" I asked. "The demon is gone."

"They don't just hunt down rogue monsters," he said. "They also target rule-breaking magic users. I'd say Mina Devlin definitely qualifies as such, so I've requested their help."

"That's good news," Jia said, overhearing. "They're going to help you find her?"

"They're based in the region next to ours, so we can cover more ground that way," he said. "We're going to search Little-wood too. I'll see if I can work with the police there."

"Good call." They hadn't known there'd been a demon loose in their village, so I didn't have too many hopes that they'd be able to handle Mina, but the more people on our side we had, the better.

Especially as Mina herself was more alone than ever, and I had her on the run. The day of our confrontation would come, one day soon... but I wouldn't face her alone.

ABOUT THE AUTHOR

Elle Adams lives in the middle of England, where she spends most of her time reading an ever-growing mountain of books, planning her next adventure, or writing. Elle's books are humorous mysteries with a paranormal twist, packed with magical mayhem.

She also writes urban and contemporary fantasy novels as Emma L. Adams.

Visit http://www.elleadamsauthor.com/ to find out more about Elle's books.